Days of
Terror

By the same author

Henry's Red Sea

Cherokee Run

Wigwam in the City

Underground to Canada

Days of Terror

Barbara Claassen Smucker

HERALD PRESS
Scottdale, Pennsylvania

Library of Congress Cataloging in Publication Data

Smucker, Barbara Claassen.
  Days of terror.

  Bibliography: p.
  I. Title
PZ4.S6644Day [PS3569.M8] 813'.5'4   79-17789
ISBN 0-8361-1910-X

DAYS OF TERROR

Library of Congress Catalog Card Number: 79-17789

International Standard Book Number: 0-8361-1910-X

2 3 4 5 JD 83 82

Printed in Canada

Acknowledgments

I would like to express special gratitude to innumerable reference librarians; to those Russian Mennonites now living in Kansas, California, Saskatchewan, Manitoba, and Ontario who told me stories of their childhood in Russia; to my grandfather (no longer living), C. F . Claassen, who worked with the refugee committees in N. America in the 1920s; to my husband, Donovan, for great assistance in research and interpretation.

To Donovan and Timothy, Thomas, and Rebecca.

Introduction

Many young people who live in Canada and the United States today have relatives who were once called "immigrants" — grandmothers, grandfathers, uncles, and aunts who migrated from an "old" country in Europe or Asia to the "new" country in North America.

Some left the old country because they needed more farm land to raise food for their families, some sailed across the ocean to hunt for gold. Many needed jobs, and others wanted fun and adventure.

There were also immigrants who sought religious freedom. In the old countries they were sometimes imprisoned and even put to death for their religious beliefs. They wanted to live in a country where they could worship as they thought best.

Peter Neufeld and his family in this story came from Russia to Canada in the 1920s seeking religious freedom. They are characters in fiction; but the story of Peter and his family did happen to many real people, and their Russian village of Tiegen (also a fictitious name) was like many villages that once existed on the steppes of the Ukraine in South Russia. Only three real people appear in the story: P.C. Hiebert, the North American relief worker; David Toews, a Canadian leader of the mass migration; and Makhno, the Ukrainian anarchist bandit.

Days of Terror

PART I: PEACE

1

A bugler's horn trumpeted melodious and clear down the dark main street of the Russian Mennonite village of Tiegen. Tall, bearded Igor, the Russian shepherd, blew with all his strength, filling the sounds from his horn with the importance of his task.

Day after day and year after year, Igor had stood before his straw-thatched hut and announced with his trumpet the exact moment between the fading of the moon and the rising of the sun when the 300 villagers of Tiegen should rise.

Now he spat into a pile of fallen leaves and shrugged his bony shoulders.

"These German-speaking people," he was thinking, "with their German names, and their German order, and their granaries full to overflowing — what has it meant that they have lived for over a hundred years on Russian soil?"

Then, just as quickly, a smile spread across the roundness of his wrinkled face and he gently hung his bugle on the wall. How could he complain? He was not one of the villagers, and yet hadn't these Mennonites paid him a wage that kept him and his old mother alive? Hadn't they made him a gift of two fine cows for his Russian village and food enough to fill himself three times a day? And had they ever beaten him? Not once. Their religion, they said, did not allow violence. How foolish. They had no guns, not anywhere.

Igor checked the sky and the coming light of dawn. Then he looked down the long wide village street and smiled again. One kerosene lamp and then another flickered orange-bright from

15

the homestead windows at the core of the village — twelve strong brick homesteads on the right side of the road and twelve on the left, most surrounded by two acres of land.

And not to be outdone, the landless villagers lit their lamps too — first the tailor, then the storekeeper, then the schoolteacher, followed by the widow who rented land and lived off the kindness of her neighbours.

Would there ever be a day — this time Igor laughed aloud — when someone among these hard working people would sleep too long and not feed their sheep and horses and milk their cows? And then would forget to lead their animals from the barn to the street where he, Igor, would herd them to the far end of Tiegen and the communal pasture? Never.

Igor loved the green pasture away from the village, where all day he could smell the sweetness of blooming clover and drink from the fresh spring water in the big round pond. He could lean against a tree and sing his sad Ukranian songs, filled with cruel misfortunes that the Russian peasant could never overcome.

In the homestead closest to the shepherd hut, ten-year-old Peter Neufeld was the first to hear Igor's bugle call. The chill of coming winter drifted through the open window of his room and sent him snuggling deep into the softness of his feather eiderdown. Outside, a red harvest sun began creeping onto the earth. After chores were done, prayers said, and breakfast eaten, the sun would be a round, warm ball.

Beams of lamplight and his mother's rustling in the kitchen were signs that he should dress at once. But he lay still, hanging onto some special joy that seemed like a dream.

Then he remembered. It wasn't a dream.

"Otto comes today!" Peter jumped out of bed and scrambled into his work clothes and thick wooden clogs. For the first time in his life he was going on a trip outside his village of Tiegen. He was going alone with Father in the spring-suspended buggy to the Russian town of Poltavaka, where his brother Otto was due to arrive at the railway station.

For two years he had not seen Otto, but Peter could remember exactly how he looked in his brown uniform with the brass buttons down the front on the day he went away, straight and tall and a little proud. Russia was at war with Germany and Otto had been drafted. Ever since then the family had worried about his safe return.

It had been a black day for the thousands of Russian Mennonites when their country declared war with Germany. Most of them lived in villages strung like green jewels along the Dneiper and Molotschnaya Rivers in the otherwise barren steppes of the southern Ukraine. Even after a hundred years in Russia, German was still their language. They had brought it with them when they fled from Prussia.

Their religious beliefs, taken word for word from the Bible, followed the commandment "Thou Shalt Not Kill." Their young men like Otto could not fight in the war, but they could care for wounded soldiers or work without wages in the forests. Otto had been an aid on a Red Cross hospital train, but now his unit had been disbanded.

From his room near the large door which connected the Neufeld house with the barn, Peter could see his small mother in the kitchen stuffing straw into the big central brick stove that carried heat from room to room. "Our Russian stove" the family called it. It warmed them in winter, cooked their food, and smoked their hams in its wide chimney.

"Ach, Peter," Mother called to him in German, "God has blessed us with the return of Otto. Bring him home as fast as Mishka will run."

They laughed together, since it was their joke that Mother liked racing in the buggy. They kept it a secret from Father who was steady and always cautious.

Peter hurried towards the heavy, wooden door that led directly to the barn. Father had already started the milking. A shaft of lamplight flickered on the giant beams above him and Peter noticed, as he always did, the date great-grandfather Neufeld had axed into the largest beam — 1805. Now it was 1917. For 112 years a Neufeld farmer had walked beneath that

17

carved date and now Otto was coming home to walk under it again with Peter.

When he came they would race each other again to fill their milking pails. They would climb into Otto's favourite apple tree at dusk and see the sun set over the strips of grain fields and the long narrow watermelon patches outside the village. They would watch the red sunset melt into the muddy waters of the winding Molotschnaya River. Best of all Otto would look at the pictures Peter drew and the borders he was designing for the Christmas poems at school. And Otto would meet his young sister, Katya, who had been just a baby when he'd left.

Peter's pride in Otto had no end. Otto could bind corn faster than anyone else in the village. Sometimes he would jump from their wagon and join the Russian farm helpers to pitch sheaves of grain.

When Otto left for the war, Peter thought constantly of his brother's trips to the battle front. He once sent a letter to Otto enclosing pictures he had drawn of Otto lifting wounded soldiers into the hospital trains while fire and bullets winged about his head.

In reply, strange letters came from Otto which were hard to understand or to believe. In the last one he had written,

> The Tsar is no longer the ruler of our country. We have no government now. The soldiers refuse to fight. They riot in the streets, and the guards of the Tsar do not protect him. They join the rioters. One result of the chaos is that our Red Cross unit has been told to return home.

There was little talk of war in Tiegen; and the great city of Moscow, where the Tsar lived, had never been visited by anyone in Tiegen. But after Otto's letter came, Father took the picture of the Tsar from their living-room wall; and Teacher Enns at the school cut all of his pictures out of their textbooks.

Grandfather Penner, his mother's father, who lived on the homestead facing theirs across the wide street of Tiegen, helped Peter understand.

18

"We know very little about the Tsar and his government, Peter," Grandfather said. "We Mennonites have lived apart from the Russian people. The price is too big to pay if we mix with them. Keeping our heritage and our faith has given us strength in a new land."

Grandfather Penner was the elder of the church and the wisest man in the village. He was old now and could not farm, but he talked with everyone who came to his home, and no problem in the village was ever solved without first asking his advice. No one feared him, for his soft white hair was gentle and his blue eyes had both sharpness and understanding.

It was from Grandfather that Peter had learned the story of the Mennonites — how in 1525 they left the state churches of Switzerland and Holland. One of their leaders, Menno Simons, had opened his Bible to the New Testament and said they should practise its teachings. But when they tried, they were imprisoned and tortured, driven from their mountain homes in Switzerland and their lowland farms in Holland. They fled to German-speaking Prussia, and again were persecuted.

One day the Empress of all Russia, Catherine II, came to them.

"Come and farm the unploughed steppes of the Ukraine," she said. "Be models for my Russian peasants. Grow grain and feed my starving people. There you can live in peace."

Great-grandfather Neufeld and the others listened.

"You may speak German in your own schools, your own churches, your own government, and you will be free until all eternity from military service. But one thing you must not do — you must not try to change the religious beliefs of my Orthodox Russians."

So great-grandfather Neufeld with his family and friends left their homes and moved in covered wagons to the treeless steppes of the Ukraine.

"God blessed us," Grandfather had said. "In a hundred years we have built more and more villages and our farmlands are called 'the breadbasket of Russia.' "

Peter checked his thoughts and swung the heavy barn door wide open. If he didn't hurry they would never get started for

Poltavaka. He grabbed his shovel from the barn wall and began cleaning the manure from running grooves behind the cow stalls. He filled the wheelbarrow and pushed it down the centre aisle towards the far door and the outside manure pile. Tall, dark-haired Father stood in one of the horse stalls brushing Mishka's smooth black hair. He smiled at Peter but didn't speak. There would be time for talk when they rode together over the steppes. Father would never say it, but Peter knew that he wanted the black mare and the spring-suspended buggy to look their best for Otto's coming home.

With the manure in its place and the shovel scraped and clean, Peter hung it back on the wall. He grabbed the egg basket and filled it to the top with warm, fresh eggs. Then he and Father nudged the barn animals one by one and sent them plodding down the lane to join Igor and the contented livestock of the village in the enormously wide main street. They waved to Igor and at last joined Mother in the warm kitchen, where the table was set for breakfast.

Father read a psalm of thanksgiving for this special day. Katya whimpered from her crib, but Tanya, the Russian servant girl, quickly soothed her by humming a sad Russian song. Tanya, with her bright flowered swinging skirt, never joined them for breakfast or morning worship. This was because of the promise to Catherine the Great.

Breakfast was eaten quickly and in silence. The hot coffee with its cold, thick cream held its warmth inside Peter. He gulped down the steaming cereal and the toasted buns called zwieback without chewing them.

"We don't eat like pigs, Peter," Father stated without even lifting his head.

Peter tried to slow the mounting impatience inside him. If Father would only hurry, for they must still change into their Sunday clothes and freshly polished shoes, and then hitch black Mishka to the buggy.

Warm sunlight now spread over the sweet-smelling acacia trees that lined both sides of the village street. It brought an orange glow to Peter's yard, brightening the flowerbeds of marigolds and asters and revealing the unpicked green beans in

the long vegetable garden. It made a bright carpet of the courtyard which had been swept clean of all leaves. All was in
readiness for Otto's return.

Across the mulberry hedge that separated the Neufeld homestead from their neighbours the Janzens, young Hans waved to
Peter and his father Henry called out, "God's blessings to you,
Peter and Brother Gerhardt." Already the Janzens had hitched
their horses to their green-flared farm wagon and were heading
down the wide street to their fields.

Grandfather Penner appeared behind the white picket fence
of his home where he lived with his deaf brother-in-law since
grandmother's death. He waved his cane back and forth for
them to see. Everyone in Tiegen knew that Peter and his father
Gerhardt were leaving at this early hour for Poltavaka. There
were no secrets at all in the village, for everyone was a Mennonite and all of them went regularly to the Tiegen church on
Sunday.

Even Igor, whose animals had already reached the pasture,
knew the comings and goings of the Neufelds, the Cornies, the
Penners, the Wiebes, the Dycks, the Reimers, the Klassens and
all the other names that twisted his tongue with their German
sounds. However, most of the other Russian servants and the
peasants, whose villages hung onto the edges of the Mennonite
towns, did not even try the foreign-sounding names. They gave
numbers to the villages. Tiegen was No. 3.

Only one farewell was left. Peter ran back into the house to
Katya's crib and woke her as he kissed her warm flushed cheek.

"Forgive me, Tanya," he said in Russian to the servant girl
who tried to scold him. "Tell her that I will bring a bright gold
toy for her from Poltavaka."

"You are a dreamer, Paitya." She used his Russian name and
Peter winced. He'd never liked the sound of it.

2

Peter rode proudly beside Father in the polished buggy. Mishka trotted with an even rhythm and his black brushed hair was a flow of rippling silk. The air was warm and filled with smells of apples, watermelons and brown-ripe grain.

Peter and Father both wore visor hats. They tipped them to the right and left as a greeting to their friends and relatives along the street. Peter called "good-bye" to Aaron Klassen who raked gravel down the long straight sidewalks before the even fences and the shading trees. Young Herman Epp and his sister Mary waved as they splashed whitewash on the trunks of their plum and apricot trees. And from the fifth storey of the Dutch windmill near the end of the village street, Jacob Voth, the miller, waved down at them as he readied the vanes that would soon flap their steady beat to the waking day of work. Finally their buggy jogged past the handsome brick school building where thin Teacher Enns was preparing for classes that would start when the harvest was done.

They neared the common pasture. Igor's baggy pants and bright red shirt waved like banners against the muted green of the trees and fields. Next they came to the narrow strips of cultivated fields. Each landowning family had 175 acres. Peter wondered that Father didn't pull the reins so he could inspect the Neufeld fields. But on this day there could be no delay.

This was the year for wheat in most of the fields. Everyone's land was divided into four sections: summer fallow when the earth rested, then winter wheat, then barley, and finally oats. Crop rotation kept the land fertile, Father said.

Because it was harvest and there had been no rains, the dirt road beneath the buggy wheels was free of ruts and bumps that often came with the slush of winter and the mud of spring. Mishka's slim legs flew with the freedom of the smooth open road and they were soon well away from the village. Peter thought how Mother would enjoy this fast run.

The steppes stretched bare and endless. There was not one tree to toss its leaves with the wind. The next Mennonite village was seven miles away beyond the far low hills.

"How fast our villages have spread and grown," Father said.

Peter knew the history of the settlements from memory . . . how the first one began on the River Dnieper in 1788 . . . how their own settlement started along the River Molotschnaya when great-grandfather Neufeld and his family arrived in 1805 . . . how today there were fifty-seven villages in the Molotschna, now the largest and wealthiest of all the settlements.

"In all of Russia how many Mennonite villages are there today, Father?" Peter had forgotten.

"Four hundred in forty-one settlements," Father answered quickly.

"And how many people in all of them?"

"Is this an examination?" Father laughed. "I imagine there would be about 125,000 people."

It seemed to Peter that their Mennonite people were blown like seeds across a prairie that wanted them to use its black and fertile soil. Someday, Peter vowed, he would see the other villages. He would go especially to Halbstadt where the Oberschulz, the elected head of the whole Molotschna settlement, lived. Otto knew him and had even stayed in his home.

Strong, hard-working Father, who seldom had many words to say, relaxed in the seat of the buggy and let the reins fall limp. He smiled at Peter and began to sing.

"Holy God, we praise They Name." His baritone filled the endless space.

At home in Tiegen Grandfather Penner would sometimes say,

"Gerhardt, with a voice of such power and beauty you should sing in the choir of the church."

But Father could be stubborn. He would shake his head of thick brown hair.

Mother understood. She would say to Peter,

"Your Father loves his farming. He is like a wild bird sealed into a box when he must stay indoors. He needs the sunshine and the fields and the wind in his face to sing."

Peter hummed the melody of Father's song as loudly as he could. The clicking of the buggy wheels caught the rhythm and even Mishka seemed to clop his hoofs in time.

In the dip of a hill, Father drew in the reins and slowed Mishka, for a tattered Russian village appeared. Its low-roofed, mud-plastered huts scattered about without a pattern on each side of the road. One of them — the hut closest to their buggy — sank into the barren earth like a hunchback. Its sagging door hung open and Peter could see inside. Around the high brick kitchen stove, a sleeping calf curled himself into a pile of dirty straw, and near him two round-faced, ragged children played.

Peter shrank back against the buggy seat at this first sight of poverty and misery. Was this where Tanya came for a holiday at home when she walked arm in arm with other servant girls away from Tiegen? There was a crumbling church with a cross on top, but even Peter noticed that the bricks were not in line.

Where was the school? He couldn't see one. Perhaps this was why Tanya could not read or write a single Russian word. Peter realized, with sudden amazement, that there was no-one among the Mennonites who could not read or write.

Peter felt sick. He had never seen a hut or a village in such dirt and disarray. Why didn't someone mend the door of the hut and sweep the kitchen clean? Why were the fields so barren and empty of food? What would the people store away for the coming winter? Surely there was little to sing and dance about in such a dreary place. Even the fences along the street, made of woven willow switches, were bent and broken. Didn't these farmers know that good fences should be made of wood or brick?

24

"Russia treats the peasants badly." Father shook his head. "The people need schools and ploughs and better food. But there is war now, and their men are fighting far from home; they are given nothing but their guns."

In a field to their left a group of peasants in baggy pants and gaudy shirts like Igor's sat laughing beneath a tree. Nearby a hand plough rusted in a weed-choked field. Father's big farm hands tensed on the reins.

"How can they waste their time in the middle of a working day?"

Peter remembered Grandfather Penner saying, "Our Gerhardt is a fine, hard-working honest man, but he's stiff as a gatepost and has no time for a good, hearty laugh."

Peter had to agree. But he liked Father the way he was. He liked his big, calloused farm hands when they lifted him from the buggy. He liked Father's straight answers that never had a "maybe." He liked his swinging steps in the wheat fields and the determination that made him finish every job he aimed to do. He liked the way Father held Katya on his lap, and the way he smiled when Mother cooked his favourite borscht. Best of all Peter liked the way Father prayed. He talked straight to God without one small apology.

Between Peter and his father there was just one thick dividing block. Father could tolerate no idleness, and Peter's drawings were not "work" to him. When Otto was at home he tried to help Father understand. Mother did not interfere, and sometimes when Peter sat with his pen and paper beneath the kerosene lamp at the large dining table, she would stop and smile over the pictures that he drew.

The shabby Russian village disappeared and the barren steppes around them stretched far and lonely into the sky. A human cry would be swallowed in this space. Only the wind roared as it blew the weird, round tumbleweeds about and filled the emptiness with unearthly moans. Peter moved close to Father.

They jogged in silence, for Father's singing had ended in the Russian village. The road now led along the shores of the winding, slow-moving Molotschnaya. Peter's uneasiness flowed into it.

Then Peter's heart skipped a beat, for in an elbow bend of the road he saw a row of stately forest trees, long strips of waving grain, and ploughed bands of rich black earth. And beyond all this was a wide smooth street with the green beauty of poplar, maple, mulberry, and acacia trees. He could see fertile gardens and laden orchards and tall brick houses with their barns attached.

It was Morgenau, village no. 4 of the Molotschna Mennonite Settlement. Aunt Helen Schmidt and Uncle Abraham lived here, but Peter knew they could not stop today. They could not even enter the village, for if they did someone would call out, "You must join us for a meal, Gerhardt and young Peter." The sight of it, however, was as good as a noonday meal.

The road had swerved away from the peaceful Molotschnaya. Father relaxed the reins.

"We will be in Poltavaka soon," he said. Peter strained forward trying to catch the first glimpse.

"It is a large city," Father said. "I was in the railroad station there once when I was a boy like you, Peter. It was clean and beautiful. The engine whistled like a great bird. There was a buffet of fine food, and men dressed in white coats poured tea, and an English lady poured cream in hers."

"Cream in tea?" Peter could hardly believe this.

3

Poltavaka could not be far away now, for the road began to fill with farmers' carts and buggies. Peter watched with growing excitement. He wanted to share each new sight with Otto, when they took the same trip back together.

But Father was confused. He slowed Mishka.

"It is not like I remember, Peter." He shook his head.

At first there were scattered neglected huts like those they had driven by in the early morning. Their gabled roofs sagged with old straw and the people outside them were ragged and thin. Dust from the road blew into Peter's face and caused Mishka to snort and toss her head.

Farm wagons and buggies jostled more closely together. Buildings were piled in rows like blocks, most of them drab, though there were a few which surprised and excited Peter with their modern designs and bright paint. In the centre of the crowd was the farmers' market, where Russian women tended their stalls, their bright head scarves matching the red apples and purple cabbages that they sold. The wheels of the Neufeld buggy began to clatter, for the dirt street had turned to cobblestones. Mishka's hoofs clicked smartly.

Not too far ahead a long train chugged and rattled to a stop near a railway station.

"Otto's train!" Father and Peter cried together.

They jumped from the buggy, pulling Mishka's reins in front of them. Father tied them to a post. He grasped Peter's hand and they pushed through the gathering crowd.

27

People of every age stood outside and inside the railway station, shoving and pushing to buy tickets at a booth. Peter saw no white-coated porters and no buffet tables filled with food. Fly-covered loaves of bread stuck from baskets here and there and spoiled remains of lunches littered the dirty station floor. People sat among the trash and covered themselves with ragged blankets.

Peter and Father stayed close together and pressed towards the train, which had now drawn in.

Then, Father saw Otto. He lifted his strong arm and waved, calling loudly in German,

"Otto, Otto, we are here!"

Peter saw him too, stepping from a car with a bundle slung across his back.

The crowds drew back from Peter and Father as though a plague had struck the two of them. One of the men pointed at Father.

"German spy," he muttered. Others gathered around him, joining in a little group of angry men.

"He should be killed," another in the group hissed.

Father and Peter didn't understand. Were they the spies? But they were Russians. This was their home.

"Death to the Germans. Death to the spies." The little group became larger and their accusations louder.

Otto ran towards Father and Peter. He grabbed their arms and quickly led them from the shouting.

"Where is the horse and buggy?" he muttered in Russian.

Peter pointed towards the post where Mishka was tied. Father grabbed the bundle with one hand from Otto's back and threw his other arm across Otto's shoulders in a gesture of protection.

Peter looked back towards the train. The man who had shouted "spies" was still crying out and pointing at them. Peter strained to hear.

"Kill them!" the man screamed. "Death to the traitors! Death to all Germans!"

Quickly Father, Peter, and Otto squeezed together into the buggy seat. A slight flick of the reins, and Mishka pranced into the street, his sensitive, high-strung nature ignited by the taunts and jeers.

"Hurry as fast as you can, Father." Otto was nervous and worried.

Father steadied Mishka and guided him carefully away from the station. Peter glanced shyly at Otto. He was taller and very thin. His uniform was rumpled and one of its coat buttons hung by a thread. Fine, little lines pinched around his eyes, telling of a deep need for sleep. But his eyes were not just tired; they were also hurt and desperate.

No more words were spoken among them until the cobblestone streets of the city ended and the miserable outer huts were far in the distance. The open steppes and the dry hot winds were welcome. Mishka settled into an even trot and Otto began to smile.

"I've dreamed of this for days," he mused. Then he turned towards Peter with his old generous affection.

"Peter, Father, we have not even greeted one another." He spoke now in the familiar, comfortable low German which the Mennonites used at home and in the fields.

Otto grasped Peter and held him tight.

"Your muscles are as strong as mine." He squeezed the steel-like toughness of Peter's arm.

But Father was in no mood for playful talk.

"Tell me, Otto, what did the shouting at the station mean?"
Otto sighed.

"It is hard to begin, Father." His voice was tired again. "The Mennonite villages have been touched very little by the war, or even by the October revolution."

"But you wrote to us," Father interrupted. "We knew the Tsar had left his throne. We took his picture from our wall."

"And we cut his picture from the textbooks in our school." Peter felt that he must add this information.

Otto was nervous and tense. "In the war with Germany there has been one defeat and then another for the Russian army. Rumours and ugly stories spread. Two million German-speaking people live within our borders; some are Mennonites, some are Catholic, and some are Lutherans. The Russians say

29

that all of us are spies. That's why they shouted 'traitors' when you called out to me in German."

Father's large, calloused hands tightened on the reins. His voice was calm and there was no hint of anger. He was puzzled and hurt.

"But Russia is our country too." Father stretched one arm in a wide arc in front of him. "We did not take this land, Otto. We were asked to come. Haven't we made our contribution? Haven't we changed these barren steppes into fields of grain that feed the Russian people as well as ourselves?"

Otto slumped into his seat.

"I've learned much at the war front, Father," he said. "Soldiers talk from their hearts when they are ripped apart by gunfire and are bleeding to death. I listened to them. There was corruption in our country under the Tsar. Wealth was given only to a few. The great masses were kept in poverty and ignorance."

"What can we do?" Father was troubled.

"It is too late for such worries now, Father," Otto answered wearily. "Without knowing it our Mennonite people have bene-fitted from the corrupt government of the Tsar. We are in between the poor Russian peasants and their former leaders. If a Civil War starts between them, they will not care what happens to us."

Peter didn't understand. Otto's head began to nod with the steady clicking of the buggy wheels, and he was soon asleep. Father and Peter sat side by side in silence.

The tumbleweeds swirled and bounced in front of them. They passed the peaceful village of Morgenau and clattered through the tattered Russian village.

A half-starved calf strolled into the road, and Mishka jumped aside to let it pass. The buggy swerved, then steadied itself. Otto was jolted awake and looked about with the jerky motions of a trapped mouse. Then he saw the Molotschnaya River.

"We are home!"

Far in the distance the green forests of Tiegen softened the harsh, flat prairie like brush strokes from a paint brush. The town spread out along the left bank of the river as it wound its slow and muddy way to the Black Sea in the south.

It was near dusk and work in the fields had ended for the day. Sheaves of cut grain were stacked in neatly ordered stooks along the fields of wheat. Plump watermelons, ready to be picked, lay fat and lazy among the shrivelled vines.

A touch of light from the sinking harvest sun spread over the long rows of acacia trees and framed the wide village street with gold. Igor in his baggy pants and high leather boots blew a welcome with his trumpet. He was bringing home the livestock for the night and waited as each plodding beast turned faithfully into its own gateway.

Otto jumped from the buggy and ran towards him. Igor took him by the arms and swung him round and round, for Otto was a favourite of his, just as he was the favourite of almost everyone in Tiegen.

At last Igor swung him free and Otto raced through the Neufelds' open gate into the clean-swept courtyard with its borders of blooming marigolds. He was there before Father and Peter arrived in the buggy. Mother ran through the large open door.

"Otto," she cried, hugging him tightly about the waist.

Behind Mother ran Tanya, flushed and laughing for she and Otto had always been friends. Toddling beside her was Katya with her red-gold curls and fat, round cheeks.

Otto stood back amazed. He was a stranger to this little girl and yet she was his sister. He held out his hands to her. Katya drew back. Then Peter came, and in an instant she rushed into his arms.

"Peter is her favourite," Mother said viewing her family with quiet happiness.

Otto drew aside and closed his eyes. Here in Tiegen he had hoped there would be no changes.

"Ah Paitya," teased Tanya switching the talk from low German to Russian, "and where is the present of gold from the city of Poltavaka?"

Memories of the city and its angry people brought a dark cloud among them.

"There is a better gift in the orchard." Peter ran along the

31

barn and behind the shed. The rows of well-tended apple trees were heavy with fruit. He chose the brightest red apple from Otto's favourite tree and racing back, handed it to Otto.

"Hold it out to her," he whispered to his brother. "She will like it better than a toy of gold."

Otto held it timidly, saying "apple."

Katya toddled towards him.

"Apple," she cried.

"Her first word!" All of the family and Tanya shouted with joy.

Otto carried his sister into the house. The cooking part of the stove was heating a pot of steaming borscht. Its potatoes, beef, cabbage, and tomatoes scented with fresh dill bubbled deliciously and filled the house with such fragrant odours that Otto stopped to inhale them with a long deep breath. On the dining table were plates of newly baked zwieback and wild plum jam, and in the centre, in the best white china bowl, was Otto's favourite dessert, Plumemoos, a fruit soup made of raisins and prunes.

"Ach Mother" — Otto smiled — "I have dreamed for two years of a meal just like this."

He strolled with Katya in his arms into the great room and stood before the white-faced Kroeger clock. The ancient heirloom, brought from the Vistula Delta in Prussia, ticked steadily, its long gold pendulum swinging back and forth as it had for a hundred years.

Otto rubbed his fingers over the blank space on the wall where the picture of Tsar Nicholas and his Tsarina had hung. He stopped to read the only other hanging on the bare clean wall:

"Lo, I am with you always, even unto the end of the world."

Through the great room door, Otto looked into the corner room where Mother and Father slept. He remembered ten years ago when he had jumped on their big wooden bed filled with barley straw and covered with a feather tick. Father had taken him swiftly to the shed and there had been a spanking he would never forget.

As they started to the dining table, Grandfather Penner

pushed open the unlatched door. He hobbled with his cane in one hand and stretched out the other hand towards Otto. He was almost as small as Mother, yet the silky whiteness of his hair set him apart as the oldest and most highly respected of all of them.

"God bless you, my Otto," he said wiping his eyes with a folded white handkerchief. He was an old man now and tears were allowed.

"It is time we should eat," Father announced.

Tanya took Katya from Otto's arms.

"Her bedtime," she explained simply.

The others gathered around the table and bowed their heads as Father prayed.

"Thank you that our family is together," he spoke firmly. "Help us to understand the troubles that Otto has seen. Keep them from us here, if it is Thy will."

4

"Today we will make watermelon syrup," Mother announced early on the first day of Otto's return. Peter and Otto grinned at one another. It was the harvest job they liked best.

The summer kitchen behind the shed was ready. After prayers, Peter and Otto would take the four-wheeled wagon to the watermelon field, where the smallest ones would be picked for mother's syrup making. The round heavy melons would be rolled into the shed and eaten fresh until frost came in late November.

Peter was glad that he and Otto would be working together,

33

for last night when they shared Peter's room near the heavy door that led to the barn, it was like sharing with a stranger. They didn't talk when they took off their clothes and were as stiff with one another as the Red Cross uniform that hung in the home-made chest against the wall.

Peter did steal quick glances at his brother.

"Otto is taller and stronger," he thought with pride. He admired the way Otto's dark straight hair was pushed back away from his forehead. He liked the short black beard that covered Otto's chin. But Otto's face was lined with worry. It stayed that way behind his smiles and laughter. He jumped at small noises.

Peter wondered if Otto was stealing glances at him. He tried to flatten his frizzled reddish hair that was just like Mother's and wished desperately for a beard like Otto's to cover all his strawberry-coloured freckles.

"I will clean the troughs if you start the milking with Father," Otto said finally. "Then we shall get started early for the melons."

Peter laughed. Maybe it was going to be alright after all. Maybe they could forget the war and the hateful people at the railway station.

"Come along, Paitya," Otto ran into the barn.

Peter flared with sudden anger but he held it silently. Why was he so angered by his Russian name?

Chores ended quickly with Otto's help. He was still the fastest worker of anyone in the family.

Mother's breakfast was a special one with fresh eggs, and Father's prayers were brief. Soon the two boys were on the wide village street in the big farm wagon with friends greeting them from every side. All the village welcomed Otto.

They drove towards the narrow bands of fields where the wheat had just been harvested. Near the winding river bed they came to the bashton, their watermelon field. In early spring Father and Peter had planted nine acres in watermelons, pumpkins, cucumbers, sunflower plants, and potatoes.

Otto stood up in the wagon, spread his arms wide and took a deep breath.

"I wish I could stay here forever, Peter."

They pulled the lush green melons from the vines and loaded them carefully in the wagon. Hans Janzen and his father Henry joined them. Peter wanted to talk and joke, but he couldn't forget yesterday. He wanted to rub from his memory the shouts of "kill", "spies", but the words nagged at his happiness. Otto said there was poverty and discontent among the peasants, that the soldiers had rioted in the streets of Moscow and wanted to kill the Tsar. He said there would be civil war. Peter knew something about the horrors of civil war. He had read in his school books how people in the same country fought each other — sometimes even brothers were on different sides.

The Neufeld box wagon overflowed by noon with a pyramid of round green melons — the magic fruit of harvest. Peter drove back to the village while Otto sat freely looking about. Father was needed in the grain harvest. He would drive home at dusk with Uncle Abram.

The village street was busy with wagons of grain being hauled to the farm yards for threshing. Other wagons of watermelons were bound for summer kitchens with their long stoves and huge hanging kettles.

The summer kitchen was Mother's workshop during harvest. She and Tanya seldom left its red adobe walls and wide open windows. Cherries, apricots, plums and apples were steamed and dried inside it — and then stored away safely for winter in the dirt cellar beneath the indoor kitchen. Katya played happily with her corn husk dolls in a grassy spot beneath a mulberry tree.

Her face flushed red from the hot brick stove that was stuffed full with straw and manure blocks, Mother greeted her sons with a quick nod. She motioned to show where the watermelons should be carried.

Katya dropped her dolls and ran towards Peter, clasping him tightly about the legs. He pretended to be bothered by her attention, but inside he warmed with the knowledge that he was her favourite.

"She does like you best," Otto said rolling the best melons near the cooking kettle and plunging a knife through the middle of them. Scoops of red fruit with slippery black seeds filled wash tub after wash tub. Peter mashed the pieces through a sieve while Otto and Tanya poured the liquid into the great cooking kettle.

Only Mother could stir the juice with her wooden spoon as it boiled. She could tell in an instant when it had cooked to a clear, dark syrup. Then it cooled and she and Tanya bottled it. These bottles too, went into the storage cellar. But tonight there would be fresh watermelon syrup for the zwiebacks!

The work had no end. The harvest this year was an overflowing fountain. What was not stored and eaten would be sold, for there must be no waste.

Peter was no match for Otto's swiftness. Sweating until they were salty wet, they worked on. The mooing of the cows down the street announced Igor and his livestock from the pasture. Dusk would come soon and then the work would have to end.

But Father had another job.

"Peter," he called loudly from the barn.

When Peter joined him he found Father with two young Russian boys, who seemed to be about his age. Their torn baggy pants and high, cracked boots told of their poverty and need.

"They are orphans and hunger has driven them to our village," Father said in low German. "They will work for us as paid labourers, Peter. We need them with such a busy harvest. Show them how to clean the barn and feed the lifestock as we would do it."

The boys followed Peter but paid little attention to his orders. They pushed at each other and the largest of the two tripped the little one and sent him sprawling into a cow stall. He barely missed being kicked.

"Die dummen Russen. You dumb Russian," Peter cried, and then regretted at once using this phrase which he and his friends sometimes said in private.

The larger boy, who was still on his feet, grabbed Peter around the head.

"You German," he shouted. "We should kill all of you like this." He smashed Peter's head into a straw pile again and again. Peter twisted and hit him savagely on the back.

Suddenly Father stood over them.

"I heard all of it," he said, shaken. He grabbed both of them by the arm and led them to the back shed. He whipped Peter first and then the Russian lad. Both boys held back their tears but there was nothing settled between them.

"You can stay if you like," Father said to the peasant boy.

The shaken lad gave the shed door an angry kick and walked out towards the village street.

The smaller boy, who had fallen into the stall, appeared in his place.

"I'll stay," he said simply and walked behind Peter.

"My name is Esch," he said to Peter. They did the milking together without a word. At supper in the kitchen with Tanya, Esch ate greedily his bowl of borscht with zwieback and fresh watermelon syrup. At bedtime, Peter led him to the loft in the barn and pitched him a fresh pile of straw. He found a clean blanket and a feather-stuffed pillow for his head. Still they didn't speak. Peter was ashamed about the whipping and felt guilty that he could not forgive the bigger boy who pushed him in the straw. He felt no remorse for the whack he had given him in the back.

What would Grandfather Penner think of him?

Peter didn't want Otto and Mother to know of the scuffle. At supper there was no word of it, and Father's evening prayers were filled only with thanksgiving for the harvest and for Otto's safe return.

But it wasn't the trouble in the barn that kept Peter from falling into exhausted sleep that night. Otto didn't come to bed. Peter could hear his soft footsteps going back and forth along their lane.

5

The joy of harvest was shattered by Otto. He became as strange to the Neufeld household as the dirty Red Cross uniform that hung apart from the work pants and black Sunday coats.

Peter saw little of him, for at night he came to their room long after the lamps had been turned down. In the fields he worked with young men his age, and when lunchtime came Peter saw him talking among the Russian helpers and waving his arms. "He thinks I am still a small boy," thought Peter in his loneliness.

Small Katya never went to Otto. She clung to Peter when Tanya was not caring for her. She brought pebbles and her corn husk dolls and laid them in his lap.

After "apple" her second word was "Peter."

"Why is she always following me?" Peter pretended disgust before the others. But then he took her hand and built her a house of broken limbs beneath the mulberry tree.

Without Otto for a friend, the new Russian farm hand became Peter's constant companion. They spoke Russian between them, and Peter wondered that the animals didn't baulk at the sharp sounds. To comfort them he called each one by a low German name. One day he heard Esch doing the same. They laughed and jumped into the haystack together behind the shed.

After this Esch began to tell Russian stories to Peter. He told of the witch Baba Yaga who lived in a hut built on chicken legs. The milk in Peter's pail spilled over the side as he listened. He

38

quickly wiped it up, for there had never been a sloppy farmer in the Neufeld family. That night after every chore was finished and Father had read from the Bible, Peter took his tablet and pen from the cabinet in the back room and sat at the dining table near the kerosene lamp. He carefully printed in fine German script at the top of the page: "November 1917." Beneath it he drew a wobbly Russian hut with gabled roof and stiff straw thatching. Beneath the hut were four spread-out chicken legs. Mother laughed so loudly when she saw it, that Father who never took one look at the drawings came to see. He frowned.

"If you must draw, Peter," he scolded, "make things look the way they are."

But it wasn't the drawing that was important that night, it was the date at the top of the page.

Otto ran in just as Father reached to turn down the lamp. His shirt was open, exposing the throbbing veins in his neck, and his brown hair lay wet across his forehead. He held a chairback tightly and gasped for breath.

"There has been a second revolution in Moscow." His voice was high-pitched and strained. "The Kerensky government has been replaced. There is anarchy in the streets, and no party can keep order. The prisons have opened their doors and bandits are rushing out to loot and kill." Otto clasped his head in his hands. "There is talk that Lenin and his Bolshevik party will take command." His voice was now wild in a way that Peter had never heard before.

A great need to help Otto filled Peter's thoughts. But the words that Otto shouted were a jumble in his mind. Who was this man Kerensky? He had never heard the name.

Father shook Otto's shoulder to calm him.

"The names of Lenin and Trotsky have been talked about in the village." Father faltered over the unfamiliar names, but his words came like a steady wind across the prairie after a lightning storm. "They say this Bolshevik party wants to take all private property. The land that we farm would no longer be ours," Father continued. "Such ideas have no place in our lives."

There was a suspended silence, broken, to their surprise, by

Mother, who seldom entered into talk about the "outside" world:

"Grandfather Penner says that this Bolshevik party will close the church doors." Mother was alarmed. "Their leader, Lenin, says religion is a drug that puts the Russian people to sleep."

Why had no one spoken to him of all these things? Peter was angered by his family treating him always as a small boy.

"Forgive me, Father." Otto looked desperately from one face to the other. "I guess I've seen too much suffering."

For the first time since his return, Otto began to talk of the soldiers he had carried off the fields into the Red Cross hospital train. He talked of legs and arms torn from bleeding bodies, of bullets that shot away one soldier's chest and robbed him of his breath until he died. He told of peasant villages he had seen that were no better than nests for rats, and of poverty that marched about the country like a hungry wolf.

Otto closed his eyes as though to erase with darkness all that was unbearable in his memory. It didn't work.

"Always when I saw these terrors — " Otto's voice was low and tight — "I thought of Tiegen and the peace and beauty of our Mennonite villages. I wanted to come home and be a farmer."

"Did you pray, Otto? Did you ask for God's help?" Father asked gently.

Otto nodded his head, and then said so softly that Peter wondered if he were the only one to hear,

"But I didn't get an answer."

"Have you talked with Grandfather?" Mother wanted to know.

"Night after night," Otto replied earnestly. "What he tells me I will never forget. But he lives only in the Molotschna Settlement. I must go to school with my old teacher in Halbstadt for a while. He has travelled and studied abroad and will be able to give me the answers I need."

Father had to make the decision for Otto's leaving. All of them knew this.

"The harvest is almost finished," he finally said. "Peter is a great help and is teaching the Russian boy well."

Peter couldn't believe that Father was talking like this about him, as if he could almost take Otto's place as a man on the farm.

"Go tomorrow." Father spoke with final authority. "But you will come home for Christmas."

"Christmas!" Otto cried. The word was uttered with relief and joy. "I will always come home for Christmas."

Peter caught the magic of the word and his thoughts glowed like the lighted candles on a Christmas tree. He began to dream that when Otto came home for Christmas perhaps they would be together again; for at Christmas time, the village of Tiegen folded into itself like the falling snow that lapped over the fences and closed the gates and the roads to the outside world.

6

Snowflakes whirled across the steppes in early November. But it was not until two weeks before Christmas that they fell in a million gentle flakes, piling one upon another.

The long, straight ditch that ran down the centre of the main street of Tiegen was sixteen feet wide. It collected water from the rains and when winter came it froze into an ice-skating canal.

Peter tied his skates tightly about his heavy shoes and when dusk came he joined his friends on the long strip of ice. He found an old pair of Otto's skates and tied them to the worn shoes of Esch. The peasant boy sprawled on his stomach at the first try — then hung with all his might to Peter's coat. Within days, they skated over the ice together.

Along the village street — to the right and the left — parents and grandparents watched from the windows of the great rooms that faced the street. Katya's nose squashed against the Neufeld frozen pane, begging to come out. "My little apple," Peter often called his sister since the day she first pronounced the word.

He left his skates dangling on the gate post and ran inside.

"I will get the sleigh from the shed and hitch up Mishka," he said to his excited sister. "Tanya will wrap you in a blanket and we will ride down the street faster than ice-skates."

There was a scurry for heavy mittens and a furry cap and a coat that buttoned tightly under her chin, and it was not long before Peter returned with Mishka and the sleigh. Immediately Katya's eyes were two dancing candle-lights.

"She thinks you are a Saint of Holy Russia." Tanya tossed the mockery over her shoulder. "Perhaps you will ride with her to the moon."

It was only with Tanya that Peter's imagination took wing.

"Yes, to the moon," he said, "but first we will hitch Mishka to the stars."

He grabbed Katya in his arms and sat her close beside him. Other sleighs passed them with jingling bells. Soft snow slid beneath them and they glided fast past the school house, then the church, and then the tiny store where Uncle Bergen baked Christmas cakes behind steaming windows.

"Faster, Peter," Katya clapped her mittened hands.

Lamplight shone from the Neufeld window when they returned — a silver pool on the smooth clean snow. Inside, Katya's cheeks were two red apples. Mother kissed their coldness.

"You smell like fresh air," she laughed, her clean blue apron fragrant with spices from the kitchen.

"Pfeffernuesse! Pepper nuts!" Katya and Peter cried together. Only once each year did the delicious combination of cinnamon, cloves, anise, molasses and other rare ingredients come together in the largest kitchen bowl to make the favourite Christmas treat. On Christmas Day there would be plates of the

42

tiny bite-sized sweets on every dining table. And if every window in the thirty farmhomes of Tiegen had been opened at one time, the winds blowing through the village would have been spice-laden and coated with molasses.

Already at school Mr. Enns had given out the Christmas poems to be memorized by each child and recited without error at the Christmas Eve program. Everyone in Tiegen, but the very ill, would be there. Even the Russian servants would stand in the hallway to listen.

Then, there would be Christmas Day when the church would open its wide doors for a celebration of songs and sermons. At home each child would place an earthen bowl in the large room, the Grosse-stube, at night and find it filled in the morning with nuts and sweets and gifts. Carollers would come on Christmas night and sing beside the Kleine-stube, or little room, windows.

Excitement mounted with each winter day, until at last it was the morning before Christmas Eve and Otto came home. He galloped into the Neufeld lane on horseback, stamping through the heavy snow. On his back was a bundle that was far too large for just his clothes.

When he opened the door, Katya ran into his arms and he swooped her into the air.

"Peter!" he called out, grasping his brother's hand. It was as though the hatred at the station, the killings in Moscow, the Bolshevik party, the bleeding soldiers that Otto carried in his arms, were no more than ugly dreams.

Peter vowed to block all of them from his thoughts for the three days of Christmas celebration. For all of them, it would be a time to renew their faith; a time to hold fast to the traditions and language which set them apart from the world, and yet held them together as a Mennonite people.

When the family sat together in a circle at dusk and sang,

> Silent night, holy night
> All is calm, all is bright

there was peace in Peter's heart. Father's baritone blended with Otto's tenor as the harmony of voices rose into a swell of unity.

All day there had been busy excitement. Tanya had gone home for the holidays to her Russian village. So Mother alone scrubbed the wooden floors to shining smoothness and baked the ham and a fresh pan of zwieback. She hid the sweets that would fill the earthen bowls.

In the barn Father and Peter, and now Otto, swept and cleaned and bedded each cow and horse with fresh smelling hay. Esch, too, had left for his Russian church and whatever friends he had in some small village.

The Neufeld family too must be clean, and water for baths boiled on the stove to fill the great barrel brought in from the barn. Father scrubbed Peter's ears and neck until they burned inside and out.

All through the day, Peter said over and over to himself the poem he would recite at the evening program. But, the best part of all would be the surprise that Peter had kept from his family. Each boy and girl at the school, in their neatest penmanship, had copied the poem they had learned. Many weeks ago these had been given to Teacher Enns, who tonight at the program would return them in beautiful covers. They would be Christmas gifts to the mothers and fathers. Peter had been chosen to design the covers for the upper grade and had settled on silver and gold for his colours. He had worked on the covers at lunchtime and after school.

Darkness came quickly, and from every home along both sides of the village street, families gathered on the freshly swept sidewalks and walked to the school. Katya was wrapped in a blanket with only her eyes peeping through, for the wind snapped with bitter frost.

All the villagers gathered in the school. When the poems were recited, mothers, fathers, grandparents nodded and smiled. This annual event brought sparkling eyes and clasped hands and tightened toes inside all the heavy, winter shoes; especially when Uncle Abram Warkentin and Uncle Tobias Schmidt entered the room with lighted tapers. A tall, Christmas tree waited for them at the front, and within minutes a hundred candles glowed in circles of gold on every branch.

Mr. Enns, with his oversized black suit hanging like shedding skin on his thin body, walked into the room with the poems in their new folders under his arm. His pupils rose at once. This was always expected when he entered the room.

Each folder was a treasure to the child who received it and Peter's covers of silver and gold with their borders of leaves and flowers and twisted lines were judged the best. Even Father smiled with pleasure.

That night in the small room beside the barn door, Otto and Peter talked together for the first time since Otto's return.

"I must stay in Halbstadt for the winter," Otto said. "I can help my old teacher in the school and keep informed about the revolution."

Peter remained silent. At last Otto no longer thought of him as a small boy.

"Remember, Peter, I'm not deserting the farm. You are a real help to Father now that you are growing."

Then Otto whispered more silently than before. "You must know, Peter, that there is great trouble in Russia. The Bolshevik party under Lenin are on the point of gaining power. Civil war is brewing. The Bolsheviks will form an army and those who want to support the old ways of the Tsar will start another army. And in between them both will be the robbers who are already starting to kill and steal because they think there is no law."

"But we have peace in our Mennonite villages," Peter answered.

"Not for long, Peter, not for long. . ." and Otto was asleep.

PART II: TERROR

7

The first present to be opened on Christmas Day at the Neufeld home was a large bulky cardboard box addressed to Katya, Peter, and Otto from Mother's Uncle Jacob Penner who lived in the state of Nebraska in America. Katya was allowed to tear off the paper and open the lid.

Inside were American Indian suits with headbands of bright feathers. Even bows and arrows were tucked beneath a special paper, and there was paint to streak one's face and a book that told of war dances with page after page of coloured pictures.

Otto and Peter shrieked with joy — and even Katya, who had no understanding at all of the contents, jumped about with excitement.

"What can he mean with such a gift?" Father frowned, not at all in favour of the war-like costumes.

"Put the costumes on in the barn," Mother advised quickly and picking up the box and wrappings led all of them out of the Grosse-stube. She returned to Father with a plate of fresh cakes.

In the barn they found Esch, huddled miserably in a pile of straw.

"S rozhdestvom Khristovym. To the Birth of Christ," he called out, using the Russian greeting.

"Why have you come back so soon?" Peter asked.

"Because I'm hungry."

"We'll soon fix that," Otto said and started for the kitchen.

But he stopped abruptly at the small window between the barn door and the house. Two horsemen, with tall hats and tattered fur-lined coats, were approaching the door of their home. They tied their horses to the trunk of the mulberry tree and pushed open the door with long sticks, for the doors in the village of Tiegen were never locked.

Otto turned to the others, for all of them could hear the banging and heavy footsteps.

"They are robbers," he said quietly, not wanting to frighten Katya, "and they are armed with sticks. Mother and Father will not understand their Russian." It was the young people in Tiegen who spoke Russian, for the law now required that they use it in their Mennonite schools.

Peter looked quickly at the Indian costumes and the frightening pictures of the war dancers in the book.

"Otto." Peter pointed to the pictures. "Let's do the war dance and frighten them away with the bows and arrows."

Otto thought for a second then gave his brother a quick look of surprise and admiration. "Yes, that's what we'll do; but we haven't much time." He took command.

"Esch," he said, "take Katya to the back shed and show her pictures in this book. She must not be harmed by the robbers."

Katya followed the Russian boy, for he was a good friend.

There was no time to look at the directions. Otto and Peter shook out the feathered head-dresses and fastened them on their heads. The fringed leather coats hung below their shirts, and they tied a string of beads around their necks. There was a small drum with two rounded sticks in the box.

"You beat the drum and shake the bells," Otto said to Peter. "I'll carry the bow and arrow. Then we'll yell as loud as we can."

They streaked paint across their faces.

"Here we go!" Otto swung open the heavy barn door.

They screamed like shrieking animals. The cows began to bellow and the horses stamped against their stalls. Even the horses outside whinnied and tossed their heads into the air.

The boys rushed into the Grosse-stube. Father had been hit across the face with one of the sticks and blood dripped from his nose. Shouting and stamping their feet, Peter and Otto raced around the room.

Mother and Father were startled. But the robbers stared with disbelief. They tossed their sticks into the air and ran for the door. Mounting their frightened horses, they plunged through the snow and into the open back fields.

The drum and bow and arrow dropped to the floor. Father slumped into the large rocking chair and Mother wiped his face with her clean, Christmas apron. Esch entered carrying Katya sobbing, into the room.

Peter wiped her tears.

"Don't be afraid, Katya," he said. "We just dressed up in the Indian costumes." He took off the feathered head-dress and Katya rubbed his curling reddish hair to assure herself that it belonged to Peter.

"What did they want?" Otto asked.

"I couldn't understand their Russian," said Father.

"The cut is not serious." Mother seemed unaware of anything else.

Father rose slowly. "I suppose I will have to thank God for Uncle Jacob and the Indian costumes," he admitted.

Peter said his own silent prayer of thanksgiving.

"Come Esch, you are hungry." Otto interrupted the serious talk, and led the small peasant boy to the kitchen. As he passed Peter, he whispered,

"Today, they came only with sticks. The next time, they will have weapons. The bandits are taking guns from the soldiers."

Peter shuddered.

That night Father locked the door of their home for the first time that Peter could remember.

Otto left early the next morning for Halbstadt, assuring all of his family that he would return soon. Christmas had healed the separation between Otto and the family, for the visit of the bandits on Christmas Day made Otto's warnings seem near and real.

After Christmas the earth froze, and the chalk gray sky brought drifting storms of snow. The gentle snowflakes were whipped together into sheets of ice.

Father pointed to the wisdom of great-grandfather Neufeld who had built their home and barn and shed together on one long connected row. There was no need to fight the storms out-of-door in order to care for the animals.

The revolution in Moscow no longer seemed so distant. Otto's letters were blunt with facts of war. They disturbed the quiet life of winter around the warm brick stove in the Neufeld home like rats gnawing into a bin of choicest grain.

Only Father seemed undisturbed.

"Haven't we built our villages with good will and mutual aid as the Bible teaches?" he said late one afternoon to Grandfather Penner as they lingered in the barn together after chores. Peter listened from his milking stool. "What have we to do with military conquests and a Bolshevik party that steals land from those who own it and have always cared for it?"

Grandfather Penner read and re-read Otto's letters.

"There is evil in the land, Gerhardt," he sighed. "Let us hope that our convictions give us courage if we are tested. When a revolution comes, men kill and plunder with violent hatred."

The story of the robbers who had been frightened by the Indian costumes spread from one end of Tiegen to the other. Friends and relatives came to see the costumes sent by Uncle Jakob, but Peter had no heart to put on the feathered head-dress or to beat the drum. The experience with the robbers was a frightening memory. He wanted to forget it.

8

It was a cold still day in February when the fury of the Revolution finally rolled into the Molotschna Settlement. Dietrich Remple, the elected head of the village of Tiegen, was in Halbstadt on matters of business. He was a big man who freely admitted that "My sin is my eating," yet there was great respect for him. In Halbstadt he witnessed a scene so horrible it was hard to believe. Wrapping himself in heavy blankets, he hitched two horses to a sleigh and started for home. He cut across fields and skimmed over wastelands, forgetting the snow-covered roads in his hurry.

In every Mennonite village along the frozen Molotschnaya River, he stopped briefly to tell his story. It was dusk when he arrived in Tiegen and the lamps were already lighted. The speed of his sleigh brought faces to the windows and all the villagers watched as his horse tramped into Grandfather Penner's lane.

Who else should the head of their village see first but the elder of the church, Ezra Penner. Peter was there helping Grandfather stack straw and blocks of manure into his fuel box.

The unlocked door swung open into the large hallway. Snow was brushed from Dietrich Remple's tall fur cap and shaken from his heavy coat that he hung onto a hook against the wall. It was no surprise to see Dietrich Remple enter the house. He and Grandfather Penner were close friends.

Grimly the large man warmed his hands at the stove and pulled a chair close to Grandfather and Peter.

"Ach, Ezra, I don't know how to begin, I have seen such a horrible thing." His round cheeks sagged over the downward curve of his lips and he rubbed his puffed, half-frozen hand over his eyes. "I don't know if Peter should hear."

"Tell it to both of us," Grandfather answered without hesitation. Peter moved closer to Grandfather. Mr. Remple began his story in a quiet, shaken voice.

"I was in Halbstadt on business, and I watched from the office of the Oberschulz. An army of bandits on horses and in carriages rode into town. They screamed and shot their guns into the air. Over one of the carriages a black banner floated. It said, 'Anarchy is the Mother of All Order!' "

Now Mr. Remple became agitated and stood as he talked.

"Their leader, a small black haired man named Makhno with a black curved moustache, rode under this banner. His carriage was polished and new and his horses were sleek and black."

Grandfather leaned forward on his cane and pulled Peter closer to him.

"What did they do?" he asked.

"They killed, Ezra; they shot six men without a trial. Three of them were teachers from the Mennonite commerce school, one boy was only sixteen, there was an estate owner, and then a young Russian lad."

"A Russian?" Grandfather's voice was almost a whisper. "Why did they kill him?"

"He cried out against the bandits, Ezra, he condemned their injustice. They shot him in the head without a word."

Mr. Remple talked now without stopping. He told of Makhno, the black-haired leader, who was as cruel and hard as a steel blade. He had broken out from a prison in Siberia, like a mad dog from a choking leash.

"Someone believes that he worked once on a Mennonite farm when he was a small boy. He carries a list of names on a sheet of paper and shouts that all of them must die. He believes in no government at all."

"God have mercy on us." Grandfather's shoulders slumped. "I'm afraid this is just the beginning."

He put his arm around Peter's shoulders. He was a small,

wiry man, one half the size of his close friend, Dietrich.

Peter needed Grandfather's closeness. The names of those who were dead had not been spoken. Chills shook his body, even with the nearness of the hot stove. His hands were icy. Otto was in Halbstadt helping in the commerce school.

"Tell us the names of those who are dead," Grandfather said softly.

The names were familiar, but Otto was not one of them. Peter slumped against Grandfather's knee with relief.

The young boy of sixteen was the son of Grandfather's cousin.

"He was a gentle boy who played a violin," Grandfather said.

"And the estate owner?" asked Peter.

Mr. Remple looked at him.

"It was your uncle, Herman Klassen." He lowered his head.

A picture of Uncle Herman rose in Peter's mind. He remembered a big man with a pointed hat and tall leather boots, who swung a cape around his shoulders and walked with long striding steps. Peter recalled the brick factory that Uncle Herman built — then the flour mill that he owned — and then the big estate that he purchased from a wealthy Russian. Peter had never seen it, but Father said there were 20,000 acres of fertile farm land with fields marked off by tile fences, and that there were brass-lined pillars for gate-posts. Aunt Lizzie, Mother's sister, lived in a fine house with Uncle Herman, her two tall sons, and her Russian servants.

Peter remembered Father saying about Uncle Herman once, "One man should not own so much." But Mother had replied, "It is not for us to judge, Gerhardt." And she reminded him how once Uncle Herman gave money for a new Orthodox church in the nearest Russian village. In return for his gift, the people of the village had to promise not to sell any alcoholic drinks for six years. She spoke also of the time when the war first came and the Tsar was still in power. Uncle Herman had given money to build a home for the war orphans and the Tsar had rewarded him with an oval medallion. It was silver and gold and was engraved with a cross and a crown and a double-headed eagle. Uncle Herman wore it around his neck.

All these thoughts spun through Peter's head. He could not believe that Uncle Herman was dead.

Mr. Remple was again talking at a rapid pace. The bandits who terrorized the city were not local people. They stole horses and money wherever they stopped, from the rich and the poor.

The Russians from the villages nearby were stunned. "Yes we want land more equally distributed," they said, "but what has happened to our country that innocent men and boys are killed?"

"They call those of us with any property at all 'kulaks'," Mr. Remple said.

Grandfather was now on his feet, pacing back and forth before the stove, punching his cane into the polished floorboards.

"God's people have always suffered," he stated in ringing tones, "but they have never been destroyed."

Grandfather's words, spoken in the warmth of his Grossestube, became like a distant wind on the barren steppes. They rolled closer and closer as the news spread and finally they were howling into the ears of all the people of Tiegen. The murdered men in Halbstadt were known by everyone.

Two days later Grandfather spoke the same words in the church on Sunday morning and went on to say:

"Pray for God's help and forgiveness if we have wronged our Russian neighbours unaware. . . . Never forget that our early forefathers were persecuted for their beliefs, but their beliefs were not destroyed."

Peter listened, seated beside Father and the other men and boys of the congregation. Father's stubbornness could be felt in the shifting of his strong, heavy body and in the clenching of his big fist.

When they walked outside, Father said to Peter and to Dietrich Remple who stood nearby,

"This judgment that is visited upon the Russian people was not brought on them by us. We Mennonites were asked to come here and we were given unploughed land without a tree, or a plant, or a house on top of it." Father looked across the fertile cultivated fields and the rows of waving shade trees. "God gave us strength to perform a miracle here. We feed the Russian people as well as ourselves. Our farms will not be taken from us."

It was late afternoon when Dietrich Remple drove his buggy into the Neufeld lane. A woman sat beside him. Her dark, straight hair blew uncombed across her face. Her wide mouth hung loose without expression. Her coat was torn and only one thin blanket covered her knees. She held a large bundle in her lap, wrapped in a thick quilt. She was tall and gaunt and as the wind drew back the skin on her face, she had the look of a skeleton.

Mother saw her first.

"Lizzie!" she cried and ran out of doors without coat or hat or heavy shoes.

"Aunt Lizzie." Peter hardly recognized her. He ran with Father to the carriage.

Mr. Remple leaned down from his seat in the buggy.

"She escaped from her home before it was burned," he said. "Not only was Herman killed but her sons also lost their lives in the fire. Lizzie was found wandering about the grounds of her estate. We have brought her to stay with you."

Mr. Remple's words were not heard by Aunt Lizzie. Her eyes recognized all of them as she looked from one face to the other, but she could not speak.

She stepped from the carriage still holding the large bundle.

"Let me take it for you," Peter offered.

When she handed it to him the quilt fell off, revealing a shining silver Russian samovar, a beautiful tea urn with a heating tube that ran down the centre of it to hold hot coals.

"It's all that I saved from our home." She finally spoke, but her words were as hollow as the heating tube of the polished urn.

Mother put her arm around her sister and led her into the house.

Peter noticed again, as he always did, how different the two sisters were. Mother's quick steps and fine featured face circled by reddish hair like his own were nothing at all like Aunt Lizzie's long, slow steps and thin, drooping face. But Peter remembered that when she smiled, as she frequently did with her wide mouth, she drew people to her with a generous, uninhibited love.

It had always been said among everyone who knew her that she was never the fine lady that Uncle Herman wished for his estate. But everyone loved her, including her Russian servants. Her tall sons and her proud husband were warmed by her good will.

"They are more human because of her," Grandfather used to say of his daughter.

Mother led the broken woman to a chair beside the stove. She removed the crooked bonnet from her head and brushed back the strands of straight black hair. She threw a warm shawl around her shoulders and Peter took off her cold, hard shoes. Father stood by awkwardly. He would give her his strength whenever she asked for it.

"You will live with us, Lizzie," Mother said. "We need you here and we need each other."

"Our terrible riches," Aunt Lizzie answered absently. "It was so much more than most."

9

Aunt Lizzie's coming changed the life of the Neufeld family. When she sat at the dinner table silently with folded hands and barely nibbling at her food, it was no longer possible to forget the revolution.

If someone asked her a question, she looked up with such pain in her eyes that Peter turned away to avoid seeing them. She could not talk about her sons or Uncle Herman. She seemed to shield them behind her eyes, not knowing how to share the horror of their disappearance. Her gaunt figure was a foreboding shadow — always gray and always silent and always sad. She worked endless hours for Mother, scrubbing the floors until there was no spot of dust. She stuffed the stove with straw and baked pans of brown, soft-crusted zwieback.

Then one day — the day of the annual horsebreaking — Tanya left the Neufeld household. Her peasant father banged at the door on a cold, dark morning, stuttering gruffly that he had come for her.

"She can't work for Germans," he said, staring at his feet.

Peter opened the door and invited him to come in. He spoke Russian better than the others in the family.

"We aren't fighting in the war," Peter tried to explain to the shabby little man. "This is our country too."

The father didn't answer, but Tanya began tearfully gathering her clothes into a bundle. Mother handed her a loaf of freshly baked bread. Peter carefully folded a picture he had drawn of her one day when she rocked Katya's crib. He tucked it against the warmth of the bread. Little Katya grabbed her skirt.

"Don't go away," she cried.

"Take care of her, Peter," Tanya called from the open door, for her father was swiftly pulling her outside. "Katya is like my little sister."

The minute the door closed the house and those inside it missed her laughter, and realised how much more they would miss her in the coming months.

"I will take care of Katya." Aunt Lizzie leaned towards the sobbing girl.

"No, no," Katya cried. "You can't laugh."

There was silence.

Aunt Lizzie sat on the floor. She pulled her long, gray skirt around her thin legs. Her wide mouth relaxed and the smile that had always before been a part of her face appeared.

"Of course, child." She rocked back and forth like a young girl. "We must not pass our sorrows on from generation to generation. You need laughter to grow."

Katya shyly walked towards her.

An invisible wave of relief passed between Mother, Father and Peter. Together they knew that Aunt Lizzie had decided, with great determination, to start a new life for herself.

Peter wondered if Esch would also be dragged away. More and more the Russian servants and labourers were leaving the village — some to join the Red Army of the Bolsheviks, and others to kill and rob with the anarchists who wanted no government at all.

Peter began to understand a long section in one of the letters from Otto.

> Our people opposed becoming part of Russian life [he wrote]. Now we are branded as well-to-do kulaks who must be destroyed. We are land owners whom they say are against the working masses. They look upon us as the rich people of Russia who trample the poor peasant under our feet. . . .

The letter was long and troubled.

Did Tanya's father want to destroy them because they owned their own farms, Peter wondered. Why did he say they were Germans?

Peter hoped Tanya would come back. He liked her lively talk and her joking and teasing; he could pretend with her and make up outrageous stories that Mother and Father would never understand. But he began to wonder if she would ever return.

Later that day, after the chores were finished, Esch called excitedly for Peter to come to the barn.

"Paitya," Esch greeted him with his round face flushed with excitement. Peter didn't mind when Esch used his Russian name. "Your Father says we can saddle-break the young horses!"

Peter's sadness at Tanya's departure was set aside for the moment and the two boys jumped up and down in anticipation. Father frowned in their direction.

"One day you'll grow out of such nonsense," he said. Already he was leading two young horses with sleek black hair from the barn. The boys followed. The weather had warmed and the ice-hard village road was soft with mud. It wouldn't hurt for a rider to be thrown from his saddle, as often happened with the frightened colts. The mud also handicapped the young horses; they couldn't run in it and kick their legs too high into the air.

The road was filled with other boys and horses. Mothers and young children appeared behind the fences. Peter saw Grandfather Penner at his gate across the road. Mother, Katya and even Aunt Lizzie waved from the front of the house. This saddle-breaking day happened each year when the early spring sun thawed the winter ice and the earth oozed with mud.

"There will be a race," Peter called to Esch as they struggled into the saddles that Father had fastened onto their horses with great care. Boys on other young horses whooped and yelled along the road. Riders fell into the mud and mounted again with dirt-streaked pants and shirts.

Finally the race was called. Peter and Esch entered together. They started at Igor's hut and ran to the gate that led into the church. The boys lined their tugging, prancing young horses on both sides of the long ditch.

Jacob Voth, the tall miller, gave the signal to begin. Peter and Esch raced together, holding their reins steady and clamping their feet tightly into the stirrups. Peter's horse shied and twisted his head in the wrong direction, and Peter knew in an instant that he wasn't a racer. The best he could do was turn the frightened animal around and lead him slowly towards their gate.

He looked down the road. Esch and Hans Janzen were ahead. The church gate was only inches away. Esch reached it first and won. Everyone cheered as he jumped from his young horse and led him into the Neufeld lane.

The attention of the villagers had been so focussed on the race that they failed to notice a long ant-like stream of armed men marching towards Tiegen. It wasn't until Igor's bugle blew that the cheering and laughter ended. A bugle call in the late afternoon was as out of place as the sun rising at midnight.

Igor was giving the people of Tiegen a warning, for by this time the leaders of the marching men were dashing into the village street. Those on horses, angered by the sticking mud, whipped their animals until blood trickled down their bellies. A few troikas careened madly from side to side as they slid into side lanes. Farmyards filled with mounted troops and wagons.

The Neufelds and Aunt Lizzie stood together in the great room of their home. Esch stayed in the barn to quiet the animals. Someone banged at the door. Until recently the person on the other side could have simply lifted the leather latch string and walked inside. But now there was a lock.

Father moved slowly towards the door. Peter watched each step. Was Father forcing himself to put one foot before the other?

Father swung back the door. Six men rushed inside as though washed in by a flood. Long dark hair flapped about their whiskered faces. Their high fur caps were slanted and cocked to one side. They seemed unaware at first of the Neufelds standing immobile on one side of the room. Their dark eyes darted over the rooms like untamed, greedy foxes. Each movement that they made clanked with rifles that hung over their shoulders and sabres that dangled from their hips.

One of them pulled out a drawer from the high wooden chest near the dining table. He flung Mother's treasured crocheted bedspread on the floor and began filling it with bedding, linen tablecloths, and napkins. He tied it like a common bag and slung it over his shoulder. Another of the men grabbed Father's fur-lined coat from a hook on the wall and threw it over his back. He paraded proudly back and forth in his muddy boots over the scrubbed and shining kitchen floor.

Peter stood with cold hands and a thumping heart. He held Katya close to him. She buried her face against his shoulder and her body shook with muffled sobs.

Father had not moved from the door. There was no fear on his face. Only disbelief. Could this rioting and disorder be happening in his house?

Mother didn't move, until one of the bandits threw the doors of her china closet open. He grabbed two of her finest glasses and smashed them against the wall. Then he saw the silverware in an open drawer and began stuffing it into his pockets. Mother started angrily towards him, but Father reached out and held her back.

"They have no respect for our lives. They would kill us like flies," he said to her quietly in low German.

Peter's attention was drawn to the smallest of the men with red rimmed eyes and thin, curled-in lips. Because he was small the others pushed him about. He was creeping towards the far corner of the room and had his eyes on Aunt Lizzie's shining, silver samovar. Peter could see that he intended to cover it with a bag which he pulled along the floor.

Aunt Lizzie saw him reach it. She strode towards him — tall and stern and as rigid as a wooden beam — and swept the samovar from him with her large, bony hands.

"It is all I have from my home," she said in a high-pitched unnatural voice.

The small man reached for the rifle inside his belt.

"STOP," Father shouted in German.

The bandits looked at him for the first time. Here was a tall, plain man with big work-worn hands wearing simple working clothes. He was a farmer like most of them. His heavy shoes were worn and scuffed. Surely he was not the kulak owner of this fine home that they had sworn to destroy.

Father turned towards Peter and spoke quickly in low German.

"Tell them in Russian, Peter, that we will cook them a dinner."

Peter cleared his throat. When he spoke his voice too was high-pitched and strange like Aunt Lizzie's. He held Katya close to him.

"If you are hungry — " Peter wondered why he was shouting. The bandits were quiet and were staring at him.

"If you are hungry," he said again, "we will cook you some dinner. I will milk the cows for fresh milk."

The bandits became gay and rowdy. The small man with the red-rimmed eyes shoved his rifle inside his belt.

"Food," they bawled. They sprawled over the room. Several pulled pillows from the bed, tearing them from each other until the inside feathers broke loose and settled in the mud that streaked over the floor. Coarse laughter and swearing followed. Peter was thankful that no-one but he could understand their filthy words.

Mother and Aunt Lizzie began building a fire in the cooking stove. They seemed relieved to be working at a familiar task.

Father moved slowly towards Peter.

"Take Katya with you to the barn." He spoke the low German words softly while looking straight ahead. "Fill the milk bucket and leave it behind the house door. . . . Take some food and blankets and hide in the attic behind the stored grain."

The bandits hardly noticed Peter as he moved to the barn door. Katya clung to him fiercely.

10

When Peter walked into the barn with Katya, he saw that it was clean and in order. The floor was swept and fresh straw was bedded in the stalls. The animals munched peacefully at the grain in their troughs. But Esch was gone!

"He won't come back," thought Peter, though he dreaded admitting this to himself. His throat tightened painfully. Esch was his best friend.

Katya became calmer. The orderly barn and the friendly

animals were a comfort to her. She was with Peter, the one she loved most in the family, and Peter had shut the door on the frightening evil on the other side.

Peter remembered a lunch that he had left in the farm wagon inside the shed. He carried Katya with him to get it. He would take it to the attic as soon as he milked a bucket of fresh milk. When he picked up the lunch, he found two zwieback that were still fresh and crisp. Katya took one of them and smiled, wiping her eyes with her blue starched apron. Speckles of dirt settled over her nose. Peter placed her in a circle of straw like a small protected bird in a nest and she nibbled at the bun patiently while he milked.

But his fingers were rigid and his hands shook. The fear inside him couldn't be stilled. The cow responded with swings of her head and tail. Peter had to shackle her hind legs together.

There were banging noises from the house inside, then more wagon-wheel sounds could be heard in the yard and gruff shouting in Russian. It could only mean that more bandits had come.

Peter began talking to himself.

"I must milk the cows quickly... Father can't leave Mother and Aunt Lizzie... I must not spill the milk... I must be patient with the cow... I must not let Katya know that I am afraid."

The banging and shouting continued from the house and yard.

What kind of men can they be, Peter wondered, until he remembered Otto's letter about the bandits released from the prisons, the poorest peasants, the beggars from the city streets.

"All of these," Otto wrote, "will not fight with either the Red or the White armies. They've banded together with a leader who tells them 'Take what you want.' "

No wonder they had come to the Mennonite villages where food overflowed in the cellars and grain attics, where the barns were filled with the finest breed of horses and cows, where the clothes were strong and well made, and where there was money and silver spoons....

At last the pail was filled. Peter carried it to the door, dipping some of the warm milk into a jar for Katya and himself. He grabbed two blankets that hung near the horse stalls and took Katya's hand. Whimpering, she followed him up the steep steps into the attic. He closed the door, but there was no lock on it.

"We will have a picnic in the attic," he said to Katya whose chubby face streaked again with tears and dust.

"I want Momma and Poppa and Aunt Lizzie to come too," she sobbed.

"I want them too, Katya." Peter knew now that she understood the terror in the downstairs rooms. Never before had either of them seen men of such greed and cruelty.

Peter cleared a way through the soft wheat kernels, the grain spread in thick layers over the floor to give warmth to the rooms below. Here and there a round green watermelon rolled from its winter storage spot. Peter found an empty corner and pushed the grain aside until he and Katya had a little wall around them. He spread one of the blankets on the floor. The other one would cover them when the sun went down and the darkness drained warmth from the unheated barn.

Katya ate some bread and cheese and sipped a little of the warm, fresh milk. In Peter's mouth, the bread was dry and tasteless.

"Will that man kill Aunt Lizzie?" Katya looked at Peter with frightened eyes.

Where had she seen a gun before? Peter wondered. There were none at all in the village.

"No Katya," he answered. "Father won't let them."

Her eyelids began to close, in spite of the fear, for she believed what he had told her.

Katya slept fitfully with one hand twisted around Peter's shirt tail. A thin crack in the thick plaster and brick wall of the attic allowed a streak of light and a cold wind to seep through. It also allowed a look-out for Peter.

He could see below into the garden plot near the barn. A jumble of farm wagons criss-crossed over Mother's vegetable garden. They had flared sides; no doubt they had been stolen from another Mennonite village. The well-fed work-horses plodded uneasily in the mud. They were used to being unhitched at the end of a day's work and led to their stalls. Several riding horses were tied to the orchard trees. There had never been horses in the orchard.

Why were the bandits so cruel and ruthless? Peter was still wrestling with the problem. He had known people in the village who were greedy and who troubled their lives with gossip against their neighbours but there was no one in Tiegen who could become so savage.

Again Peter thought back to the letter in which Otto said that the bandits lived such miserable lives that they knew no right or wrong; that when the Revolution emptied many of them from the prisons, they had to steal in order to live. "These people have never settled anywhere and planned for the next generation as we have," Otto wrote.

Peter remembered Otto's description of the gold-domed Russian churches that threatened the poor peasant with punishment if he didn't put coins in the money boxes. Now these miserable people had a leader named Makhno who preached murder and robbery. "All the love has been squeezed from his soul," Grandfather had said, "and he is filled with revenge and hatred and greed."

The noises from the house below shifted to the barn.

"We'll have that horse, and that one, and those cows there." Peter heard a hoarse voice shouting out the orders in Russian.

"Leave the farmer one cow and that crippled black horse."

Could he mean Mishka? Peter trembled. Mishka was old, but a good horse. He could never pull the plough for spring planting. He had never been a work-horse.

Through the crack in the wall Peter could see two men laughing in the yard with mulberry jam running over their black whiskers. They carried Mother and Father's barley straw mattress between them and dumped it into one of the farm wagons. Another man threw Aunt Lizzie's hand-embroidered tablecloth over the back of his horse. He wore Father's fur coat and carried Father's Sunday jacket with the high black collar over his arm.

"Take some hay from the barn," one of the men shouted.

Peter froze. What if they came for grain in the attic? He

pulled the blanket over Katya and prepared to hide under it if the door opened.

Darkness came out of doors and closed in the attic like a sealed box. Peter could see nothing — no shadows, or shapes, or even outlines. It made no difference if he closed or opened his eyes.

He drew Katya closer to him and tucked the blankets more tightly around both of them.

Loaded with all the goods they could carry from the Neufeld home as well as the cows and three horses from the barn, the bandits stumbled onto their horses and into their wagons. Peter could hear the clattering of the wheels go down their lane and out the gate. Noises now came from the wide village street. Was the ant-line of tramping men forming again to wind its evil way over the steppes and then on to another Mennonite village?

Peter wanted to shout for Father. He wondered if Mother and Aunt Lizzie could be locked in the cellar or tied together in the empty stalls of the barn.

At last the door at the far end of the attic creaked and then opened.

"Peter!" It was Father whispering.

"I'm in the corner," Peter whispered back. "Katya is asleep."

Father had no light but he knew the room well enough to creep around the edges. Peter held out his hand and Father clasped it. Warmth and relief poured through Peter like a flooding stream. He wanted to fling his arms around Father and press his face against Father's cleanness and goodness.

"They have gone now, Peter," Father said calmly, "but it is best that we not light the lamp. Give Katya to me and we'll go down the stairs.

Smouldering embers from the hay inside the cooking stove dimly lighted the kitchen and the dining room. Food was spilled over the floor and onto the sides of the polished dining table that Great-grandfather Neufeld had made more than a hundred years ago. Broken glasses and dishes scattered beneath their feet. The white-faced Kroeger clock ticked loudly on the wall and the Bible verse in gold and black letters showed with such clearness that it startled Peter:

"Lo I am with you always, even unto the end of the world."

Mother grasped Peter in her arms and held him close. Aunt Lizzie kissed sleeping Katya on the forehead and Father laid her on the sleeping bench and pulled it near the stove.

At another time, the disorder of the rooms would have sent Mother scurrying for her broom and pail. Tonight this didn't matter. Their family were together and they had not been harmed. Father drew a circle of chairs around the stove and opened his Bible for evening worship.

"I have chosen Psalm 27", he said and began to read.

"The Lord is my light and my salvation;
    whom shall I fear?
The Lord is the stronghold of my life:
    of whom shall I be afraid? . . ."

As he read on, Peter heard mostly the words that said "do not be afraid." Perhaps Grandfather Penner, Father and Mother and Aunt Lizzie could do this, but he was afraid.

"We will pull what beds are left into the Great Room tonight and sleep near the warm oven." Mother's briskness was automatic. "Most of the blankets were stolen."

Aunt Lizzie began sweeping the debris from the floor.

A small rapping sounded at the door.

No-one spoke. Peter's heart pounded so loudly that he pressed his hand to his chest to quiet it. Father opened the door slowly.

Jacob Voth, the tall miller, entered the room. Blood ran from a cut on his forehead. Aunt Lizzie sat him on a chair and wiped the cut clean with a wet towel. All of them gathered around him.

"I have gone from house to house," he said weakly. His short beard, usually white with flour dust, was caked with blood. "It is the same everywhere. Our barns have been emptied. Our bedding and our clothes have been stolen. In some homes they took all the money they could find."

"Was anyone hurt?" Father asked.

"Yes, Tobias Schmidt was shot to death when he stood in front of his horses and tried to keep them in the barn," he answered dully.

Tobias Schmidt, whom the whole village knew as Uncle Tobias, always lighted the candles on the Christmas tree at the school, Peter remembered. How could they shoot such a kindly old man?

11

The village was in chaos. Some of the houses were empty, for the families who lived in them fled to safety in the homes of relatives or into the summer kitchens hidden in the orchards.

Grandfather Penner could not be found, and the old brother-in-law who lived with him refused to talk.

"He has gone to his friend, Dietrich Remple, I am certain," Mother concluded.

Two days later, a polished black droshky pulled by two white horses clattered down the village street. The Neufelds watched from their large front window.

Five Soviet officials sat in the four-wheeled carriage as stiff and upright as the tall black hats on their heads. Long swords protruded from hilts that were fastened to a leather belt around their waists.

"Nothing good can come of this," Aunt Lizzie commented dryly.

"It's safest to remain at home, Gerhardt," Mother pleaded with Father who was already putting on his coat to go out.

Father hesitated, and then paced back and forth before the window.

Peter stood beside him. It seemed to him that they waited for hours watching an empty street. At last they saw Jacob Voth running down the street towards the church. He was always the first to see events in the village from the top of his windmill.

"I will wait only thirty minutes more and then I will join him." Father checked the Kroeger clock on the wall.

Peter watched the long gold pendulum swing slowly back and forth. Thirty minutes had almost ticked away, when miller Voth came running into the Neufeld lane. He was out of breath when Father opened the door for him.

"Grandfather Penner was taken by Soviet officials to the prison in Melitopol!" he gasped. "He was taken in a buggy stolen from his barn."

"Why was he taken?" Mother grabbed Jacob Voth's arm.

"What did he do?" Father was shocked.

"Grandfather is the elder of our church." Peter was confused. "People are arrested when they do something wrong."

"I saw it happen." The tall miller sank into a chair; his face was pale and drained of all colour.

"Tell us everything." Aunt Lizzie stood grim and unmoved.

"Our local self-government has been replaced by a local Soviet — a counsel of workers and peasants. Five of them came today wearing uniforms that fit them badly. The leader is a man who cannot read. They will make all decisions for the village of Tiegen."

The Neufelds and Aunt Lizzie were stunned. Jacob Voth talked faster.

"Grandfather Penner, who was at the home of his friend Dietrich Remple, saw them drive their new droshky into the church yard. He strode down the street to the church and stood before the door.

"The five new officials marched up the steps of the church.

" 'What do you want here?' Grandfather demanded.

"The new leader of the local Soviet sneered. He is a big man with a loose chin and a moustache that is as long as a tree limb under his nose. He threatened Grandfather with the tip of his sword. But Grandfather would not move.

" 'I will have my assistant read to you why we are here,' the big official shouted, adding a stream of curses that hurt my ears."

Jacob Voth covered both his ears with his hands and sank back into the chair as though he had been beaten.

"And then what happened?" Aunt Lizzie demanded.

"They called him a crazed preacher and a wealthy land owner," the miller began again. "Then the small assistant stood in front of Grandfather and began to read from a paper. It was loud enough so that all of us in the church yard could hear. He said,

" 'The Bolshevik government has made this law. The church has lost its place in our society. Its property has been nationalized. It belongs to the government. We will have our local Soviet offices in the church.' "

Father stood with his mouth open. He couldn't speak. He started for the door, but Mother pulled him back. "We must hear all of the story first, Gerhardt."

Jacob Voth put his hand to his head as though struggling to remember what had happened next. He went on.

"Grandfather still would not move from the door. 'You will have to kill me first,' he told them calmly, 'before you enter this church.'

"Then the big man laughed and told his assistant to read again from the paper.

" 'Since we have all authority in Tiegen,' he read, 'We are demanding a tribute of two million rubles.' Then he said, "You will be held as a hostage in the prison at Melitopol.'

"Then three of the Soviet officials grabbed Grandfather by the feet and the arms and dragged him into the buggy. They rode away down the village street."

"Two million rubles!" Mother was appalled. "It is impossible to raise such a sum."

If the miller had taken a hammer and pounded them one by one over their heads, it would have been no worse than the pain and horror of this news. The shock of his words filled them with a greater emptiness than the robbery of their food and clothing.

"Grandfather's old brother-in-law ought to stay with us," Father said. "Sit here, Jacob, and I will try to persuade him. And when I return I will go to the church and I will talk with the new Soviet officials."

"Then you will also be taken as a prisoner." Aunt Lizzie spoke bluntly.

"Aunt Lizzie is right. She knows about their cruel ways, Gerhardt." Mother said with pleading in her voice.

Peter's head ached with all the talking. The closing of the church . . . Grandfather a prisoner . . . a new government in Tiegen. Why didn't Otto come home? Peter yearned for his brother. No-one else seemed to help him understand.

A black cloud fell over the Mennonite villages in the weeks and months ahead. It was a time of howling storms made up of human voices. Lightning struck at the village in the shape of guns and swords. Many were killed. Thunder banged at the doors. Sometimes the noise came from the Red Army, trooping through their towns. But then the battle lines changed, the Soviet officials disappeared, and it was soldiers of the opposing White Army who marched, marched, marched down the village streets. The most violent of the thunderings came with the bands of anarchists who whipped themselves into living demons.

Peter and his family lived from day to day. They were thankful when there was some food left in the cellar and some grain in the attic. They were thankful that one milking cow was still in the barn, and thankful that they were yet unharmed.

Their picket fence lay broken along the ground and the sturdy front gate was a pile of splinters. Mishka pulled the plough for the vegetable garden, and no-one went out to the distant grain fields. The winter wheat was starting to grow tall but there would be no farm machinery left to harvest it. It had all been stolen.

When the local Soviet government made its office in the church, Dietrich Remple, the village elder, had no place on its staff. Father refused to enter the church building now that it was defiled by a group of soldiers. But one day he stood before

73

the open door and spoke loudly against their use of the church as an office. He also told them that they should be gathering the wasting harvest. The large man with the long moustache shook his fist at Father and threatened to shut his mouth forever by sending him to the labour camps in the frozen north.

But Father refused to listen to him. He demanded to know when Grandfather would be returned from prison. They laughed at him.

Peter stood in the churchyard waiting for Father, expecting him to be shot. But Father plodded down the church steps with his big farmer's hands dangling without purpose from his ragged sleeves. He took Peter's hand and they walked home together.

These days Father often went to see Igor in the shepherd's small hut at the end of the village street where no bandits ever came. Why the sad bearded Igor had not fled long ago to his Russian village, no one knew. But the people of Tiegen were pleased that he stayed. Igor and Father were becoming friends. They were blunt but honest with one another.

Together they plodded each week from one end of the village to the other finding those who had the greatest needs and those who could give them help. Often Peter went along. Father walked into the houses and Igor into the barns. Their shoulders sagged at the end of such a day but they became one of the binding links that held the village together. Father's sober honesty and unbending faith formed a sturdy wall to lean upon. The local Soviets viewed him as a peasant, big, simple, and rugged from labour. They joked at his awkward Russian speech, but otherwise left him alone. Igor loved the animals that had been under his daily care. He mourned over the sickly lot that were left in the stables. Each evening now Igor came to the Neufeld door for a hot dinner. Mother and Aunt Lizzie never failed him, not matter how meagre their fare.

The stove became a prison cell for Mother and Aunt Lizzie. Day after day one set of soldiers and then another banged at the dining-room table. "Slaughter the chickens — Bake us some bread — Give us some borscht thick enough to chew — Fill it with meat.''

74

Unwashed, they gulped and tore at their food. The surplus of fruit, vegetables, and meat in the cold storage cellar shrivelled. The grain in the attic scarcely covered the floor.

Peter milked the lone cow and tended poor Mishka. His shining black coat was dull now and covered with scars. There was little for him to eat and his bones became knobs pushing at his skin. His mouth folded back from his teeth.

Peter also cared for small Katya. Whenever the soldiers or bandits banged at the door, he ran with her to the attic or to the summer kitchen behind the orchard. To Katya, Peter meant safety and refuge. She clung to him.

One day Peter saw from the window a ragged troop of bandits run through the village street with Red soldiers close behind them.

A bullet struck thin teacher Enns in the cheek, and he came to their home for Mother and Aunt Lizzie to tend him. There would be scars for the rest of his life, but his eyes, mouth and nose had not been touched. For this he was thankful.

There was no school for him to teach, but he lived on in the teacherage next door. No one raced through his house to steal. He had little to offer but books, which he carried lovingly from the school and stacked for safety in the Neufeld storage cellar.

"You may read any of the books," he said to Peter who sat with Katya at the wide dining table.

"I am teaching Katya her numbers and her letters in both German and Russian," Peter said, and teacher Enns pondered at the young boy's aged appearance and soberness of his responsibility.

"Sometimes Peter draws pictures too," Katya said. "He drew a picture of last Christmas when we were riding in the sleigh." The little girl moved closer to her brother.

"Peter cares for the child, because Lizzie and I are constantly at the mercy of the soldiers to cook for them," Mother explained wearily.

"Well perhaps I can find a little more paper for you to draw pictures," said Teacher Enns. Already all the paper in the house had been written and drawn upon in every direction — in the corners, forwards and backwards, and then crosswise — so

Peter smiled eagerly. The hunger in his mind for books and paper matched the hunger in his stomach for food.

A week later Father had an idea. He learned that many of the housewives were bringing whatever valuables they could find to the village store to be exchanged for food.

"Perhaps we could spare some butter and cream," he suggested to Mother and Aunt Lizzie. They agreed. In the store where the exchanges were made Father had seen two treasures that he had thought to get for next Christmas. But now he felt the children needed something to lift their spirits. And who knew what would be left in the store by next Christmas?

One of the treasures was a porcelain doll made in Germany. Her eyes closed with long lashes and her real hair spun over her head in a halo of gold curls. Father wanted her for Katya. There had not been much joy for this small daughter who stood beside Peter white-faced and shaking when the soldiers came. Her only toys were her corn husk and cabbage leaf dolls.

The other treasure was a notebook of smooth white pages that had writing on only one side. When Father first told Mother about the notebook, she smiled for the first time in months.

"Peter can use the clean pages for his berry juice drawings!"

"They seem like a waste of time to me," Father answered, puzzled. "But to please you, Marie, I will get it."

Mother grabbed his hand and squeezed it warmly.

Storekeeper Bergen made the trade for Father without questions. He smiled at the unlikely scene of big Gerhardt Neufeld wrapping a doll and a book in a torn blanket and pushing them carefully inside his thin, frayed coat.

It was the quiet time of dusk in the Neufeld home that evening and the family sat around the dining table, waiting for Father to read from the Bible in front of him. Katya leaned against Peter, twisting nervously at one of her braids. Her face was drawn and sober.

"It's a hard time for children," Father said, looking anxiously at his small daughter. Then he reached under the table for the bartered gifts that were rolled into the tattered blanket.

He handed the china doll to Katya.

The red light from the stove flashed on the porcelain face of the beautiful doll and made it seem life-like when he handed it to Katya. Her eyes were wide and unbelieving as she stretched out her arms for it. She rubbed one small hand over the golden curls. She tipped it back and forth as the eyes opened and closed.

"It is mine," she laughed hugging the doll close to her. "I will call her Lizzie."

Aunt Lizzie's gaunt face broke into the wide smile that had been locked away since the robbers and soldiers started banging at the Neufelds' door. For the first time since he had known her, Peter saw tears running down her sallow cheeks.

Peter held the notebook that Father slipped onto his lap. The blank pages in it were clean and smooth. He could hardly wait to dip his pen into the berry-red ink and draw fresh pictures.

12

The presents helped, but the worries persisted. The absence of Grandfather Penner preyed on all their minds. His empty house became a tomb, for the old brother-in-law hid himself in the barn and ignored the robbers as though they were insects not worthy of his recognition. The rooms of the farm house were empty and the windows were smashed. Mother, Father, and even Aunt Lizzie went time after time to the new Soviet officials to ask of his welfare.

"When can he come home from the prison?" Mother pleaded with them for an answer.

Aunt Lizzie spoke out more loudly. "Why can't you bring

him home? He is an old man, he had done no harm. The tribute that you ask for his return cannot be paid. Our money has been stolen." The tall, gaunt woman had no fear of these officials. They could not add to her suffering. They were uneasy in her presence.

But they never had answers. Peter thought of Grandfather's faith in God and hoped that he could bear his hardships.

The closing of the church was like a death-blow to the people of Tiegen. Pouring stones into the water wells would have caused no greater alarm.

"How can we live without our church?" Mother said over and over.

"We will keep our faith alive in our homes." Father's large hands became tight fists. "If our Bibles are taken from us we can repeat the verses from memory. No one can steal our faith. No sword can cut off our silent prayers." Father spoke quietly, but with such determination that Peter felt drawn to his words as though to a life-or-death emergency.

The Neufelds with Aunt Lizzie joined hands in a small circle. There was a moment of silence and Father ended it with "Amen." It was like making a pledge to one another, Peter decided. God could be worshipped even if the church was closed.

The school had been closed even longer. But there were rumours from the local Soviets that it might open soon. The government and not the church would be in charge. There would be no courses in religion and no study of German. The new teacher would be a Russian.

"But Teacher Enns is our teacher," Peter and his friend Hans Janzen protested.

"They will not only ban religious instruction," Aunt Lizzie said, "but they will teach against it."

"This could never happen." Mother leaned her head against the bricks of the big stove. Sun streaked across her face and the tight curls of her hair. Peter was startled by the sudden illumination of a hundred tiny wrinkles creeping over her face. He could see her as an old, old woman. Her reddish hair, now matted and dirty, was the colour of dust. It had been so long since they had had combs or brushes or soap.

Had all of their family changed so much?

By now it was early summer and the heavy front door stood open to the sunshine. But there was little of the happiness of previous summers. The yard was rutted by wagon wheels, and unkempt. Broken fence posts, smashed hedges and untended trees littered the ground from one end of the village to the other. The soil was sour with dead roots. Peter suddenly remembered Esch and the good times they had together. But it was Katya who held his hand. She seldom left him. When the bandits came, it was Peter who protected her.

"Maybe there is still time to plant crops, Gerhardt," neighbour Janzen, Hans's father, called from his side of the broken mulberrry hedge.

Father smiled and walked to greet his friend. It was good to see a familiar face and talk about the hope of planting. Mother called to her best friend, Lydia Janzen, whom she hadn't seen since Chistmas.

But their greetings were interrupted.

Jacob Voth, the miller, ran towards them. He was breathless and flushed.

"I heard it from Igor who has just come from Lichtenau. The train has stopped there with hundreds of German soldiers. They will occupy the Ukraine! Some of the Mennonites in Lichtenau greeted them with zwieback and slices of ham. A few even sang 'Deutschland, Deutschland.' They welcome the soldiers as protectors!"

"One army is as bad as another." Father was grim. "The whole world seems to be at war. How simple it would be if the soldiers would put down their guns and beat their swords into ploughshares as the Bible teaches."

"I wish it could be that simple, Gerhardt." The miller was thoughtful. "The Soviet officers say that the Russian army is falling apart and that the Bolshevik government has signed a separate treaty with Germany. They have given all of the Ukraine to the Germans."

"It is of no importance to me what they do." Father was finished with the discussion. "The Bolshevik government is an evil one for our people."

Peter wanted to know more. He would have to find the miller Voth later in the day.

"Perhaps they *have* come to protect us," Mother sighed.

There was little time to prepare for this new army. Two days later they could be seen marching beside the winding Molotschnaya River and into the wide street of Tiegen. The young German soldiers could not believe what they found. In the depths of the Russian Ukraine were village after village of German-speaking people.

One of the soldiers stopped at the Neufelds' broken gate and picked up Katya, who now wore long red-gold braids.

"My little sister," he laughed. "And look, she holds a German-made doll."

The day before the local Soviet officials had vanished on horseback and in buggies. And this time even Igor had plodded slowly out of the village with a bundle over his shoulder.

Father had tried to stop him. But he only looked up sadly and walked on.

"It is not good," he mumbled, "to be friendly with the enemy. It will only bring more hatred from the Russian peasants. You forget that I am a Russian and a peasant. I have not thought of you before as Germans."

Peter wanted to make him stay. He was leaving like Esch and Tanya. Why must his three good friends just walk away because of the war?

A new kind of order came to the village. There were soldiers in the village homes again, using their beds and eating their food; but this time the people talked and laughed with them. When they weren't drilling with their guns, they mended the fences and helped plough the gardens.

Weeks passed, but Father, along with others in Tiegen, was

not at ease with all that happened. There were guns, loaded and stacked, againt the walls of their homes. For almost 400 years there had been no guns in a Mennonite home.

Father became harsh with Peter when he marched with the other boys of the village beside the soldiers as they drilled. He openly disagreed with one of the orders.

"The Russian peasants shall return all that they have stolen from Tiegen," an officer had ordered. "If they refuse they will be shot."

"I do not want any of my goods returned at the point of a gun." Father stood squarely before the German officer to emphasize his words.

But there were a few among the Mennonites of Tiegen who were eager for the return of their stolen cows and horses and silver spoons. They received the goods without a question.

Gardens were harvested that fall and a few crops grew in the outlying fields. Hardly anyone, however, turned the fallen leaves into the soil for better moisture and better growth as had been done by Tiegen farmers since the orchards were planted.

Mother made watermelon syrup in the summer house and stored it in the cellar. There were small sacks of grain for wheat flour and she and Aunt Lizzie piled the dining table high with zwieback. Peter didn't tell anyone, but night after night he picked ripe apples from the wide-spreading tree in the orchard and hid them in the unused summer house stove.

Fall passed quickly. Then the winds began to chill the air and there were warnings of snow in the cold, gray clouds. The German soldiers became restless.

"It is an uneasy peace," Aunt Lizzie finally said one night at the close of family worship. "The guns and the drilling can't rebuild our village. Something evil seems to be blowing in the wind."

A knock at the door came like an answer to Aunt Lizzie's fears.

It couldn't be the soldiers, who would walk in unannounced.

"A stranger?" Father went to the door.

It was Igor!

The old shepherd smiled wistfully, but his eyes were filled with fear.

"Listen to me." His Ukrainian words became a wail. "The war with the Germans is over. They have lost. An armistice has been signed with the great nations of Europe and North America and the German soldiers will leave Tiegen tomorrow. But our civil war in Russia will go on and on. The Red Army is angry and the bandits have joined them. The White Army still fights to bring back the old government of the Tsar.... You Mennonites have been friends with the enemy. Who will protect you now? No-one!"

He trembled even as he sat by the warm stove.

"You were friends with the enemy." He shook his head. "Thousands of tramps, and beggars, and gypsies, and peasants have joined the bandit Makhno. They swear revenge on the Mennonite villages. They talk of killing and burning your homes and your barns."

Katya began to cry and ran towards Peter.

"Take her to the barn, Peter," Father said gently. "The cow must be milked and Katya can help you."

The little girl ran for her doll and held it tightly against her.

"The bandits won't kill Lizzie," she said soberly. "I will hide her in the barn."

"The child knows the truth. We can't keep it from her," Aunt Lizzie said with her usual bluntness.

"But we must shield her as best we can." Father's answer was quick and without hesitation. Mother agreed.

Peter left with Katya at once, but he knew that he must not be shielded. He had to know what was happening. He was not a child like Katya. He left the barn door slightly ajar so he could hear all that was said inside the house.

Soon there was another rap at the door and then the clipped German-speaking voice of Officer Schmidt.

"Perhaps you know what has happened," he said crisply. "We are withdrawing our troops at once." He paused to unstrap the gun from his shoulder. "You and your family, Herr Neufeld, will be in great danger from the Makhno bandits and the Red Army."

"Our good friend Igor has just told us." Father was alarmed.

"You must have army rifles for your protection," the officer said. "I will give you two, one for you and one for your son."

Peter was tempted. He wanted to rush into the room and say "yes." He had learned to shoot with the soldiers at rifle practice.

There was a long silence and then Father spoke out clearly.

"It will be hard for you to understand," he said to the officer, "but for almost 400 years our people have held to the Bible teachings of peace and non-resistance. 'Thou Shalt Not Kill' is one of the Bible's commandments. Our forefathers suffered for the right not to bear arms."

"But Mr. Neufeld, if you can't kill, take the rifles anyway. If the robbers know you have rifles they will stay away." The officer spoke with urgency.

Father shook his head. "If they come in spite of the rifles, I'm not sure what I would do. I am only a human being. Would I be strong enough to overcome the temptation to kill if the rifles were standing in the corner?"

The officer shuffled his feet with embarrassment.

"You should know, Mr. Neufeld," and now he was impatient, "that many of your young Mennonite men have organized Self Defence (Selbstschultz) units in the villages. The German army has given them arms and trained them."

"God forbid!" Father spoke out loudly.

"They have pledged themselves only to practice self-defence," said the officer, trying to soften his announcement.

"Where have they organized?" Father demanded to know.

"The largest group is the First Halbstadt Company. It is made up mostly of senior students from the Halbstadt School of Commerce."

The Halbstadt School of Commerce! Peter could hardly believe this. Otto must be one of the group.

"My son Otto is in that school," Father said hesitantly. "Do you know if he is a member of this Self Defence?"

"Otto Neufeld?" The officer spoke the name with familiarity. "Yes, of course; he is one of the leaders."

"You may go now." Father's voice broke but he was firm.

There was tense silence inside the house. "That's why we haven't heard from Otto for so long," Peter thought, and returned to his milking. He watched Katya lay her doll in a horse trough that was no longer used. She covered it carefully with straw and then draped a worn horse blanket over the top.

"Lizzie will be warm and she won't be frightened," Katya whispered to Peter.

13

The departing German army, the paralyzing fear of new invasions by the bandits with a fresh revenge to urge them on, and now the announcement of a Mennonite Defence Unit with Otto as one of the leaders spread gloom and fear through the Neufeld household.

Supper was eaten in silence until at last Father said, "Peter, you should know that Otto has joined an army."

"I know, Father, I heard the officer tell you."

"I must say this and it is hard" — Father's big hands spread over his black Bible — "I believe that a Mennonite who surrenders the idea of peace and affirms war is no longer a Mennonite."

"We must hear what Otto has to say," Mother pleaded.

"There is always forgiveness, Gerhardt," Aunt Lizzie added.

Peter felt that his heart might break. What would it mean if Father no longer thought of Otto as one of them. He had wanted to take a gun too. What if the robbers came again to shoot at Father, Mother, Aunt Lizzie, or even Katya? Would he welcome Otto and his Self Defence? Were they really an army if they did not invade a town to steal land and food and people?

But the commandment that Moses had carried down the mountain from God weighed heavily on Peter's mind.

Peter remembered Grandfather Penner saying, "If you began to kill you become like those who are trying to kill you. Those who love God practise brotherhood." But what kind of people were Makhno and his bandits? Were they human? If only Grandfather would come home. Peter could talk with him.

At worship that evening, Father read the Ten Commandments and the Sermon on the Mount from the New Testament where Jesus told them to love their enemies; but he also prayed for Otto.

"You must pray for Lizzie too," Katya demanded.

Father smiled and closed his eyes and prayed for the safety of Katya and her doll, Lizzie.

When he finished he placed his hand on Peter's arm.

"We have work to do in the barn," he said to the others. "Katya, you help Mother and Aunt Lizzie."

In the growing darkness of the barn, Father spoke with urgency.

"You are growing up, Peter; we must work together now."

A happiness spread through Peter that he couldn't explain. How could he be happy with so much misery on every side of him?

"There is no longer hope for our Mennonite people in Russia, Peter." Father spoke the words cautiously. "Our homes and our barns are in ruins, our land is being taken from us, many of our churches are closed, and our school will soon teach against religion... and now our young men are fighting as soldiers!"

Father was raising his voice. Peter looked carefully around to be certain that only the cow and poor, tired Mishka could hear.

"Our Mennonite leaders are talking of mass migration. We are seeking a new country where we can live as a Mennonite people and keep our faith."

"Leave Russia, Father!" Peter couldn't believe what he had heard. How could they leave their home where great-grandfather Neufeld had chopped the date 1805 into the ceiling beams with his axe? How could they leave Tiegen where he and

Otto would be the fourth generation of farmers to live in this sturdy brick farm house?

Father was serious. "A committee of our leaders have gone to the United States and Canada to talk about mass migration. But when the Soviet officials return we must not let them know of this."

"Do Mother and Aunt Lizzie know, Father?"

"Yes, Peter, it is the one hope now that we are living for. But the children are not being told."

So at last Father no longer thought of him as a child.

"I will only talk with you about it," Peter promised.

Father became tense.

"The bandits will return, Peter. Let us pray that we will survive, but we must protect ourselves as best we can."

Peter agreed.

"Tonight we will all sleep together in your room near the barn. If the bandits come it will be easier for you to escape with Katya to the summer house or the attic."

Peter listened carefully.

"When everyone is asleep, I plan to take the bricks from the lower corner of the warming oven and hide most of the money we have left there. It will be needed for passports and travel. Only you must know, Peter. Mother and Aunt Katya might be forced to reveal the hiding place."

Peter tried to stop his trembling. He wanted to be a helper, not a coward.

Father placed a steady hand on his shoulder. "Take care of little Katya. She is so small. Make a better hiding place in the attic and in the summer kitchen."

Peter thought of Katya's doll.

"The stuffing is coming out of Katya's doll, Father," he said. "Why don't I take it apart and fill it with money, then sew it up again? A bandit would never steal a doll, and besides she has hidden Lizzie in the horse stall."

"A good idea, Peter." Father smiled briefly over Katya's hiding place.

At suppertime, Jacob Voth, the miller, appeared whitefaced at their door.

"I am going from one house to another with the news." His body was stiff like one of the vanes on his windmill. Peter wondered if he could move unless the wind pushed against him. "A traveller from western Taurida has brought word that Makhno and his bandits have crossed the Dnieper River and are near the Sea of Azov. It is said that there are 20,000 men and that they plan to attack all 57 Mennonite villages of the Molotschna. They say we gave support to the enemy and that our Self Defence Companies killed many of their men."

The cold wind that blew through the open door could have been a sheet of ice. Peter was frozen and little Katya's hand, as it grabbed his, was an icicle.

Only Father moved to close the door as the miller Voth backed away from it. Father drew all of them near the stove and placed a bundle of fresh straw inside it. They pulled their chairs around it in a half circle.

"I remember a song that I used to sing when I was a small boy," Father said. "I want to sing it now."

Peter thought he might whisper the words, but instead the fullness of his deep baritone burst forth as though he were in an open harvest field. It could surely be heard from one end of the village street to the other.

"If Thou but suffer God to guide thee
And hope in Him through all thy ways.
He'll give thee strength what-e'er betide thee,
And bear thee through the evil days."

Father finished the song and then said quietly, "I am not afraid."

Peter felt relief and warmth pour over him like steam from Aunt Lizzie's samovar. Father had taken away some of the fear from all of them. Peter knew the words of the song too. He would remember to sing it again and again when there was need.

They began to make plans. They would sleep fully dressed in

the back bedroom near the attic stairway. Peter and Katya could escape to the attic where food and blankets were stored in a far corner.

"I will answer the door alone when the knocking comes," Aunt Lizzie insisted. "It is the man of the house that they shoot first."

Mother tried to protest.

Aunt Lizzie laughed. "When they see my long face and my big feet and hands I will frighten them more than they will frighten me."

Then she grew serious. "I will feed them at once until they are drowsy by the fire. You must only come out of the bedroom if there is fighting."

"You are brave, Lizzie." Mother said. "We will try it."

Father hesitated, but finally agreed only if there was no violence.

For three days the village was quiet. But the Neufeld family and Aunt Lizzie continued to sleep together in the small bedroom. On the fourth night after Jacob Voth's announcement of the coming invasion, Peter's sleeping was filled with dreams. They were about Otto, who carried a sword and a helmet and whose eyes were red like flames of fire. There was yelling and shouting, and then he woke.

There was still yelling and shouting.

"Carry Katya to the attic, Peter." Father was speaking to him and it was not a dream.

Peter stumbled up the stairs. Katya was heavy for she was still asleep. He took her to their corner hide-out and covered her carefully with a blanket.

The shouting out-of-doors came from across the village street — from Grandfather Penner's empty house. Peter looked through the crack in the wall.

The sight was like another horrible dream. Makhno's bandits were gathering around Grandfather Penner's barn. Their long black hair twisted like snakes biting at the wind. Some of them wore pointed caps with a red star on the top, for they had joined with the Bolsheviks. A shining black droshky carried the leader, Makhno. Thick pillows were stuffed behind his back.

He leaned forward, shouting and cursing fiercely. Here and there torches were lit and then hurled one after another into the tall haystack near the barn. There was an explosion of light. Peter could see the faces of everyone in the crowd.

Strands of burning straw blew from the haystack over the barn, covering it with rims of light. There was a crackling sound and the barn was on fire. Shouts erupted from the bandits. They pranced their horses around the blaze, pulling at the reins so tightly that blood dripped from the animals' mouths. The old deaf brother-in-law, who had refused a chance to stay with the Neufelds, came running from the barn door.

Peter saw the leader Makhno lift his rifle and aim directly at the bewildered old man. The brother-in-law jerked up into the air, then fell and was quiet. He was dead.

It was the first time Peter had seen a man killed. He began to cry with great sobs and had to cover his face with a blanket to keep from waking Katya.

The crackling sound grew louder. The flames spread. Now the house was on fire, glowing like a thousand lanterns into the exposed rooms for the front wall crumbled away like falling blocks. For an instant Grandfather Penner's empty rocking chair could be seen near the Russian stove. Then it burned in a roar of flame.

The light from the fire seemed brighter than the sun. It excited the riders and the horses and they raced around the burning farmstead in a drunken celebration.

Peter looked at Katya's calm, sleeping face. If the bandits set their barn on fire, he would take her at once down the stairs and out of the shed door and then run to the summer house in the orchard. He began folding his blanket for such an escape.

The Neufeld home was untouched on the night of the great fire. But the kindly storekeeper, Isaac Bergen, was shot to death when he had no cakes to give away. And the home of Aaron Wall, one of the landless villagers, was also burned to the ground.

Night after night the bandits came. The plan in the Neufeld

home seemed to be the best they could work out. Aunt Lizzie greeted the drunken bandits when they hammered at the door. She led them to the fire and fed them hot borscht.

"Where is the man of the house?" they would bellow while eating their food.

"He is dressing," she would say. "He will be here soon."

Then they would fall asleep and leave when daylight finally came.

One night Aunt Lizzie's plan didn't work. Two bandits came who were not quieted by the food or the comfort of the fire.

"We must see the owner, or we will burn down his house until he crawls through the flames."

Father whispered to Mother, Peter and Katya. "I am going to help Aunt Lizzie. I will blow out the lamp and seize their guns. Run to the summer house."

Peter wrapped a blanket around Katya.

He could see Father stride into the dining room.

"I am the owner of this house." He grabbed the bandit's gun that was aimed at Aunt Lizzie and pushed it up so that the shot exploded into the ceiling.

"Run to the summer house," he cried to Aunt Lizzie in low German.

He blew out the lamp on the table and the room was black.

There was shouting and scuffling and another shot.

Within moments Peter, Katya and Mother were in the summer house and Aunt Lizzie joined them.

Then, there was a thudding sound of running footsteps. It was Father. His ear was bleeding and he carried two guns. He hurled them far back into the weed-filled orchard. Mother tore the apron from her dress and wrapped it around his ear. It had only been nicked by the bullet.

"The bandits have left for this night." Father was exhausted. "They are cowards without their guns."

14

It was now full winter again. Snow came with its soft flakes announcing Christmas. But the school was closed and the church was a building to be feared. It held the local Soviet government that could tax, or divide land, or take animals and food, or imprison, or even kill without a chance to protest. There was no sugar for pfeffernuesse and no Christmas ham to be baked. And Otto would not come home.

But at least there was a blessed respite from the soldiers and roving bandits.

"The ice and freezing winds must be keeping them close to some far-off campfire," Mother sighed wearily.

Despite their worries it *was* still Christmas, and Peter and Katya shared a small secret. Teacher Enns had kept his promise and had brought them paper.

All the pencils in the house were worn down to stubs, but Peter found a box of penpoints. He coaxed Mother to boil more berry juice until it thickened into a dull red ink. Because the house was quiet, Peter and Katya sat at the dining table pretending to learn letters and numbers. Instead, Peter wrote Christmas poems and designed the edges of the page with flowers and birds and curls of leaves. Katya filled in the blank spaces with her own pen and pot of berry juice. Peter began to teach her a Christmas poem. They would celebrate Christmas after all.

At last it was Christmas Eve and Mother and Aunt Lizzie cooked borscht. They used the last cabbage from the storage cellar and dipped spirals of sour cream over the top of it. Peter and Katya placed a polished red apple on everyone's plate from their secret storage bin in the summer house oven, and under each plate were the carefully printed Christmas poems with their dull red berry-juice borders. Aunt Lizzie dropped hot coals one by one in the heating tube of her samovar. She made Russian tea with its piping hot water.

Father opened the Bible and read the story of Christmas and said a prayer for the safety of Otto and Grandfather Penner. Mother began to sing "Silent Night, Holy Night" and the others joined her. The wind howled out of doors but the big Russian oven with its burning straw warmed them and each one smiled with memories of other years.

Then the door blew open and Igor entered, shaking the snow from his hair and beard.

"S rozhdestvom Khristovym," he said smiling, surprising them all that he even remembered the blessed season in these hard times. It didn't seem to matter that there were no gifts for Peter and Katya. The family still had each other, and now Igor had joined them.

But the peace of Christmas disappeared like a melting snowflake.

Word of the outside world came from Igor. Some said that he could put his ear to the ground and hear all that was done and said in a radius of a 100 miles. Peter looked at him with awe at all the news he collected and the predictions he made that usually came true. "The Self Defence Company fought with the Makhno bandits," he told them one night. "One Mennonite was killed."

"Was it Otto!" Peter blurted out with anguish.

"No," was the only answer.

For weeks Peter thought there would surely be some further news about Otto. Father would not talk about the Self Defence, and Mother and Aunt Lizzie did not urge it.

Then one night, three months later, Igor came to their door again with news from a distant place. His hands were shaking and his eyes were wild.

"The bandits joined forces with the Red Army and their combined armies have overwhelmed the Self Defence Units by the thousands," he shouted. "The Self Defence has collapsed and are disbanding. Many were killed! All of their lives are in danger!"

"If Otto is still alive, his danger is much greater than ours," Peter thought. They had each other and Father's great faith in God's help. But what if Otto did escape to their home. Would Father refuse to let him in?

There was no time to ask this question, for a loud banging shook the door.

Igor slipped away into the barn like a disappearing shadow. Peter and Katya ran for their attic hide-out. Mother, Father, and Aunt Lizzie stood near the door.

It was the bandits again. The oaths and shouting were more raucous than usual. Every word could be heard in the attic. Katya held her hands over her ears and clung to Peter.

The men below cried out their orders in Russian. "We have two men sick with typhus — put their beds near the stove — give them tea and sponge their heads — don't let them die."

Then there were no more words from the bandits — only the moans and the delirium of the two sick men.

"Typhus!" Peter heard Aunt Lizzie shout. Her Russian speech was filled with German words but she could make herself understood. "It's a plague more deadly than the death from your guns."

The typhus, brought on by filth and constant hunger, spread from house to house in the Mennonite villages like a tumbleweed blowing across the steppes. It brought fever and thirst and delirium — and if one recovered it left a weakness that crumpled one's legs and arms.

That first night Peter finally slept, with Katya in his arms. But when he woke off and on during the night he could hear the voices of Mother, Father and Aunt Lizzie below.

"Take more of this tea," Mother was saying to one of the sick men.

"How can they be so filthy?" Aunt Lizzie's voice held disgust. "What chance is there to fight a disease when fleas and lice creep from the hair on their heads to the toes of their feet?"

"They are men who need help," Father said patiently. "But we must keep Peter and Katya from the sick men. The disease spreads like fire. They must stay only in the back room, the attic, or the barn."

One evening while Mother bent to sponge the head of a sick bandit, she fainted. Father carried her to the small back room near the barn. Aunt Lizzie followed close behind. She loosened the collar of Mother's dress and placed her hand on her feverish head.

"She has the typhus too." Aunt Lizzie bit her lips. "The disease knows no boundaries."

Father's hands dropped helplessly to his sides.

Peter knocked at the door. Katya was busy in the barn hiding her doll Lizzie in a dark corner where the hens once laid their eggs.

"The house is cold and there is no more straw to burn in the stove," Peter told Father who opened the door. "Hans Janzen is chopping down a tree in their orchard for firewood. Maybe I shculd cut down the pear trees that didn't bear well."

In days before the Revolution such an act would have been a sin to Father. One did not destroy a tree that bore fruit. But now the world was in a somersault, Peter sometimes felt. It was hard to see things straight or in any kind of perspective. Each day was met with the desperate need for food and warmth and safety and Peter wondered if God could hear Father's prayers.

Father didn't hesitate about chopping the trees.

"The house must be kept warm," he agreed. "I wonder if I would have the strength myself to chop hard wood. What would we do without you, Peter? See that Katya stays in the barn."

Peter hurried from the sick room to the barn.

"Brush poor Mishka," Peter urged his small sister as he walked to the tool shed for the axe. This was a job she had just learned and it pleased her as well as the ageing horse.

How did it happen that the bandits hadn't taken the axe, Peter wondered. He would hide it in the summer house when he finished with the pear tree. There would be at least two more months of cold weather. Other trees would also have to be used as fuel.

Striking the axe became a rhythm and Peter found that swinging it up and down warmed him inside and out. He hit harder and harder at the leafless tree until floods of bitterness surged inside him and seemed to rush through his swinging arms into the splitting woods. He hated the men who pounded at their door night after night. Why must they curse and steal from his family? Why must they point their loaded guns at Mother and Aunt Lizzie? Why must they destroy the beautiful village of Tiegen?

He was exhausted and weak when the pear trunk at last lay in short logs over the ground. He could barely pick them up and stack them. Hunger overpowered him. He hoped there would be hot food for supper.

Peter decided to go to the summer house at once and hide the axe. When he crawled through a small secret opening, he cried out sharply. A man was huddled in the corner rolled in a blanket. He was asleep. He didn't look like a bandit, yet it was hard to tell. His boots were cracked and his hair and beard were matted with mud. His coat was ripped at the shoulder.

Peter crept closer and looked into his face. It was Otto! Peter grabbed him by the shoulders and shook him.

Otto sat up at once, startled.

There was instant recognition and the two brothers hugged each other with relief and joy.

"I'll call Mother and Father at once," Peter said. "You must come into the house."

"No, Peter." Otto pulled him back with alarm. "How much do you know about me and what I've been doing?"

Peter told him everything. What Igor had told them. What Father said. How Mother and Aunt Lizzie answered him. He told him about the bandits and the typhus and about little Katya. And he told him too about the money hidden under the bricks of the stove and the money stuffed in Katya's doll. He told Otto of his fears and his desire to support the Self Defence army and at the same time hold firm to their Mennonite beliefs.

The words poured out of him the same way the anger had poured out and made him hit the tree trunk harder and harder with every blow of his axe.

Finally Peter was exhausted. In his need for Otto's help, he had forgotten that his brother was thin, and dirty, and hungry. The strong, tall Otto whom he had seen last had changed into a tattered beggar. Only his eyes were the same. They were still thoughtful and kind.

"Listen to me carefully, Peter," Otto whispered as though listeners might be in every corner of the summer kitchen. "I am in great danger. The Red Army has vowed to kill all members of the Self Defence. If Father or Mother see or know that I am here, they will be accused of giving me aid. They would be shot too."

Peter knew that every word was true.

"At first our Self Defence pledged only to protect ourselves and the villages from the Makhno bandits. The bandits vowed to destroy us when the Germans left." Otto hunched low into his worn coat and did not look at Peter. "Our Halbstadt Company launched a surprise attack on them near a village they planned to seize. Forty of them were killed and only one of us."

Peter couldn't believe that this was Otto talking.

"We ran out of ammunition, Peter, and the White Army helped us keep Makhno at bay on two fronts."

"Yes." Peter was breathless.

"Then the Makhnovites joined the Red Army and we were outnumbered by the thousands. But we resisted the Red Army! We were no longer just a local militia trying to protect ourselves. . . . You can see my danger, Peter."

"Yes," Peter answered again, not sure that he understood everything but wanting to hear more.

"Now we have disbanded." Otto's voice was low. "Many of our men were killed, some of them joined the White Army, and some like myself have gone into hiding."

"Father says, Otto, that it's the first time in four hundred years that Mennonite men have used weapons and gone to war."

"That is right Peter. It was a terrible decision."

"Where are you going now?" Peter needed to know for Katya might call him at any moment.

"I am travelling by foot and pretending to be a poor Ukranian peasant on my way to visit relatives in the south. Thanks to the servants on our farm, I speak the Ukranian dialect like a native. My hope, Peter, is to reach the Crimea and stay with friends in one of the Mennonite villages there."

Otto felt inside his torn coat pocket.

"I've written the name and address on this paper, Peter. Hide it where no one will see it. In two or three months write to me about our family. Put the name of my friends on the letter, not mine."

Peter took the paper and stuck it far down into the sole of his shoe.

"How can I help you now?" Peter asked.

"See if you can find a pair of my shoes and anything warm that won't be missed. Bring them to me here." Otto paused.

"I'm hungry, Peter. Is there any food at all that can be spared?"

Peter reached at once into his secret hiding place for the apples and filled Otto's hands with them. They laughed. The apples were proof that once there had been an abundance of food and once there had been peace and laughter at the very place where they now sat together.

Katya called from the barn.

Peter jumped up to answer her.

"I'll be back Otto. I won't tell anyone that you are here."

Mother was very ill. Aunt Lizzie tended her constantly while Father did what he could to care for the feverish bandits.

Peter knocked lightly on the barn door. He was still forbidden to enter the house for the typhus germs were everywhere.

Father came out, stooped and haggard.

"I've brought the logs, Father." Peter hoped that the sight of the neatly split wood would cheer his father a little.

"Bless you, Peter." Father bent to pick them up. "Mother needs the warmth.... I have a gift for you, too."

On the table behind him were two loaves of freshly baked bread.

"The widow Sawatsky uncovered some hidden grain. It is an answer to prayer. She is sharing her bread with all of us." Father handed one of the loaves to Peter. "You and Katya must have one loaf in the barn and we will share the other in the house."

Peter was joyful. Half his loaf would be given to Otto.

"And Father" — Peter needed to get the shoes and the warm clothes now — "it's cold in the barn without heat from the stove. Could I use Otto's warm jacket and heavy shoes and the blanket that is hidden in the storage chest."

"Of course, of course." Father's distractions with Mother's illness made him unaware of the valuable garments that he was handing out so readily. In a moment he returned with the shoes, the jacket and the blanket and handed them to Peter.

"Pray for Mother, Peter, and take good care of Katya." He closed the door.

In the barn Katya was still brushing Mishka. The old horse half closed his eyes with pleasure.

"After you Peter," the little girl said without stopping her brushing, "I love Mishka best, and then Aunt Lizzie and Mother and Father."

"And Mishka loves you too," Peter assured her.

He spread out their supper of fresh bread and milk and slices of apple. They ate hungrily. Just chewing the whole wheat grains in the bread was a pleasure.

Peter put their blanket for the night near Mishka. If he was in the summer house with Otto, and Katya wakened in the dark, she wouldn't be frightened with the faithful black horse standing by her.

It was dark before his small sister finally slept and the lamps were turned down inside the house. Peter crept quietly into the orchard with the precious items under his arm.

Otto was sitting up waiting for him.

Peter was glad it was dark. When he heard his brother's voice he could imagine that he looked exactly like he did before the war and the Revolution.

"I asked for the shoes and the jacket and the blanket for myself," Peter said breathlessly, assuring Otto that Father had no knowledge at all that he was there. "He is so worried about Mother, that I could have asked for the Kroeger clock on the Great Room wall and he would have given it to me."

"Freshly baked bread." Otto said the words like a prayer. He rubbed his long slim fingers over the loaf. Then he tore off a large piece and stored the rest in a bundle. He broke each bite with special reverence and then gulped the fresh milk that Peter had carefully carried in a cup from the barn.

"Tell me, Peter," Otto finally said when he had finished eating. "Do Father and Mother and the people of the village talk at all about the future."

Peter remembered Father's words about the mass migration. He had hidden them away in his mind for he didn't want to think of leaving home.

"Mass migration!" Otto stood up with excitement and eagerness. "Then there is still hope that we can save our Mennonite faith."

Peter couldn't follow his words.

"Where do they talk of going?" Otto asked.

Peter had to think hard to remember. "I've heard them talk of Mexico, the United States, and Canada."

"Canada and the United States." Otto seemed to treasure the words, storing them away in his mind as the precious clothing and bread had been stored in his bag.

"Now I must sleep, Peter." Otto hugged his brother warmly. "If you hadn't found me, I might not have been able to stay alive. Take care of our family. I will pray each night for all of you, and for Grandfather Penner if he is still alive.... And remember, Peter, when you write to me don't use my name on the envelope. Use the names of the people on the piece of paper."

There were scuffing noises near the house. Peter turned to go, fearing that more bandits might be coming. If they were

Katya needed him more than Otto.

"I'll be gone before daylight," Otto called as he left.

The noises ceased and Peter rolled into his blanket beside Katya and the ancient horse and went to sleep.

In the morning when Peter woke and tried to open his eyes, his head thumped with pain and his lips felt as thick as rising zwieback dough. He saw Father coming into the barn from the house. Then his mind blurred. Soon there were shadows of Aunt Lizzie bending near him with water. Words faded off and then on in his ears....

"There is no soap left to wash the germs from their bodies," he heard.... "There are no clean clothes"... "There is no medicine"... "Katya has the typhus too."

The kerosene was gone and the lamp smoked and puffed with sunflower seed oil.

15

The plague swept from village to village, creeping along through the dirt and filth that the bandits left wherever they went. Many of Mahkno's men died in the beds which they occupied in the homes of the Mennonite people. Long ago they had stolen all the sheets and towels.

It was a miracle that the Neufeld family survived, and that Father and Aunt Lizzie did not get the disease at all. One of the bandits died and his body was carried to the village graveyard. The other one was taken by his family to a distant village. Even Igor managed to nurse himself through the plague alone. He came to the Neufeld home emaciated and pale.

"I am hungry," he said simply, his long black hair falling over his shoulders. "I have nothing left to eat."

By another miracle, Mother had managed to hide a large sack of millet. She was still too weak to stand at the stove, so Aunt Lizzie cooked it slowly and put it into steaming bowls and poured fresh milk on top of it.

Peter and Katya were still ill, but they could now sit up in bed.

"I want Lizzie," were the first words Katya said.

Peter crawled weakly to the barn and uncovered the doll from her hiding place.

Aunt Lizzie scolded him for going to the cold barn as she brought the bowls of millet to their bed.

"It is the best food I have ever eaten." Peter scraped the last bite from his bowl.

"I want some more." Katya held out her bowl.

But there was no more. There were lean days ahead for everyone in Tiegen and all food had to be rationed.

Igor stayed after eating for he had news to share of the plague.

"Forty bandits and soldiers died of the typhus in Tiegen and were buried in the village graveyard," he told them. "Among the villagers who did not live were Dietrich Remple and his wife and poor Aaron Wall, whose house was burned to the ground."

The Neufelds were numb with so much suffering. They could not even respond. But Igor did not stop with his sad news.

"The Ukraine is drying up with drought," he wailed. "The winter wheat that was planted is blowing out of the ground and flying away in the wind. The roots are shrivelled against the seeds. It is not just here, but there is drought in all of Russia!"

Could Igor put his ear to the ground and listen to all of Russia?

But Igor's words were true. There was drought and famine in all of Russia. The bandits and soldiers were no longer a menace, for the typhus had been a greater killer among them than their guns and cannons. Those who recovered left the village. There was nothing left to pillage.

The fertile land around Tiegen that had produced food as though from an overflowing fountain was now parched and cracked and blowing with dust. It, too, was starving.

The Red Army of the Soviets was crippled with hunger and the new government declared a time of recovery if only the rains would come. They might even allow the Mennonites to own and work their own land again, they said.

So it was a surprise to everyone when two army policemen came to the Neufeld house early one morning.

"We have an order to arrest your son Otto. Is he here?" They were sharp with their questions.

"Otto!" Mother rose from her chair near the stove. She walked slowly towards them, for her strength had been slower to return that that of the others in the family.

"Is he near? Has someone seen him in the village?" She was eager and excited.

She didn't hear them say "arrest." Peter was sure of this, but as he lay in bed he began to shake as though he had a chill. The address of Otto in the Crimea was in his jacket pocket.

"Stupid woman." The officers turned abruptly away from the door. "She thinks we're returning her son to her." They mounted their horses and rode away.

Father helped Mother back to the rocking chair near the stove.

"If they are looking for Otto, then we know he is alive. That is some comfort."

Surely if Father and Mother were glad to have Otto alive, they would forgive him for joining the Self Defence. Peter wanted to believe this. He would add this to the next letter he planned to write to Otto as soon as he found a clean piece of paper.

Peter found it hard to walk when he finally left his bed, and little Katya seemed no more than two large blue eyes on a small white face. Only Father was strong enough to carry in the logs that Peter had chopped, and build a daily fire. Mother shivered with cold "to the bone," she said, and sat by the stove constantly. Aunt Lizzie, though, appeared untouched by the typhus. She worked steadily as though wound up like a clock.

"I don't need as much food as the rest of you," she said abruptly. "I had too much for too long." This was the first time since she lived with the Neufelds that she mentioned her life with Uncle Herman and their sons on the large estate.

Peter and Katya were so weakened that they could do little but sit by the stove. One day Peter thought of the books Teacher Enns had stored in their cellar. Aunt Lizzie carried them to the dining table. He began to read. "At least I can fill my head," he thought, "and forget about my empty stomach."

Sometimes he read aloud to Mother and Aunt Lizzie who stitched frayed garments and re-knit stockings that no longer had soles.

"Draw a picture, Peter," Katya begged. Peter dipped his pen in the darkening juice and hunted for a blank space in his criss-crossed notebook.

To make her laugh, he drew a picture of Esch falling on the ice the day he learned to skate. But the pictures they both liked best were the ones he drew of watermelons, apples, and loaves of brown wheat bread.

There was still millet to cook and a small portion of milk from the bony cow. After this was gone everything conceivable was eaten, whether or not it was nourishing. But always they shared what they had with Igor. Peter's stomach burned as if it held glowing embers. All of them drank far too much water. Every morning Father brought out the scales and weighed out what passed for bread. It was as black as the earth and as hard as rock. Mother and Aunt Lizzie made it from material swept out from the corners or between the boards in the barn. This wheat and dust was ground on the coffee mill and stirred together with water and home-made yeast, and then baked. Tears ran down Father's cheeks as he doled out half a slice to each of them. One day it was all they had to eat.

It was a desperate day when Aunt Lizzie cooked field mice and the bodies of crows that swarmed in the barn yard for stray kernels of grain. Peter swallowed the food with closed eyes. The taste didn't matter; he needed something inside him.

The warm summer days brought more and more people out of their homes and into the villages seeking food. A ragged group of Russian children collected beside the window of the Neufeld dining room on a day of bright sunshine.

"Bread! Bread!" they cried in Russian.

Father looked at the empty table. He walked to the window to draw the shades.

But Peter pushed them aside. Esch was in the group!

"I see Esch!"

No one could stop him as he opened the door and pulled his small friend inside. They were shocked by his appearance. His face was shrivelled like a small dried potato.

Mother lifted the cellar door and reached for a cup of precious milk. No one uttered a word of protest, not even Katya.

Esch sat among them.

"Drink it very slowly," Mother warned. "Drink it sip by sip with this spoon."

After the last spoonful, Esch leaned back wearily against his chair.

"I will take him to his place in the barn," Peter offered.

Aunt Lizzie lifted her hand in protest, then dropped it helplessly.

"All of Russia is starving," she said. "We are united in our hunger."

Esch curled up to sleep in some fresh hay that Father had managed to collect.

"How do you still have a cow, Peter?" The lively mischief that once shone from the Russian boy's eyes was gone.

"Father manages to keep it somehow."

"The cow will dry up like everything else," Esch said.

"I missed you when you left." Peter tried to talk as though

the time that separated them was only a week.

"You are my friend, Peter," Esch said closing his eyes. "I came here because you are my friend."

He curled up in the hay and fell asleep. Peter covered him with a heavy blanket.

The next morning when Father and Peter came to the barn to milk the bony cow and feed Mishka, they found that Esch was dead. They placed his small body in a wooden box and buried it in the barren orchard.

"Let the young boy's soul find peace," Father prayed over the mound of earth.

Peter wept bitterly.

"Let's not tell the others," Peter said. "There is so much sadness already.

"Satan himself seems to have entered what was once our Garden of Eden," said Father summing up the years with sadness.

The future looked dark and hopeless.

PART III: DELIVERANCE

16

A time of despair came to Tiegen and the other Mennonite villages. Instead of the noisy, shrieking terror of the soldiers and the bandits tramping into their homes and through their streets, there was now the quiet unseen terror of drought, disease, and famine. Month followed month with no relief. A full year passed and life became as fragile as a stalk of straw. All of Russia suffered, and the children who lived, lost forever the growth and strength that food could have provided.

In the Neufeld home in Tiegen, Peter pulled the plough that Father guided and they had a small garden in the summer. The lives of the people in the starving villages slowed to a creeping pace. There was little energy to walk, or to lift, or even to hunt for food. But through the long days of the famine the villagers of Tiegen shared with one another. There was never enough food, but there was always some.

One morning, however, there was nothing to eat in the Neufeld home. The thin, bony cow had stopped producing milk weeks earlier, and when Father went to the barn at sunrise, he found that the starving creature had died. No one was surprised.

Father and Peter still talked about the money hidden beneath the bricks and inside Katya's doll. There was little mention of mass migration these days, for no one could think beyond the need for food. But even the money was useless. There was nothing to buy.

"I will walk to the next village," Father said one day.

"Perhaps things are better there." He looked about the room desperately, tying his wooden clogs onto his feet with strips of cloth from a worn apron.

When he opened the door there was a stir of noises outside. Village people were walking down the sidewalk to the school.

"There is a meeting in the school," Jacob Voth, the miller, called to the Neufelds. Peter, Katya, Mother and Aunt Lizzie snatched their coats and shawls to join him. Father walked by his side.

"It's hard to believe," the miller said, "but a man has come from the North American Mennonites."

How tired and ragged we look, Peter thought as he entered the schoolroom with his family and sat on arranged chairs and benches. There was little joy as neighbours and relatives greeted one another, and yet there was a tightened air of excitement, like an unexpected light from a dry lamp wick.

A tall man in a black suit with combed brown hair and gold-rimmed glasses walked to the front of the room. Uncle Abram walked with him, and Peter noticed that his arms were too long for the short sleeves of his thin coat.

"Brother Hiebert has come to us from North America," Uncle Abram told the hushed assembly of neighbours. "He will speak, but first he asks that we pray the Lord's prayer together."

Softly, in whispered words, "Our Father who art in heaven..." Then with swelling entreaty, "Give us this day our daily bread...."

The villagers of Tiegen could go no further.

Mr. Hiebert wiped his eyes.

"Reports of your need and suffering have reached the Mennonites of the United States and Canada," he said slowly. "We have received written permission for relief activities in the Ukraine from the Central Committee of the Soviets. The need for food in all of Russia has caused the formation of an international relief administration. Help is on the way."

Katya pulled at Peter's sleeve.

"What is the man saying?" she asked fearfully, her large blue eyes circled with deep shadows.

Peter leaned down to her.

"He says that the Mennonite people of Canada and the United States are going to send us food."

"Food?" Katya questioned, hardly daring to believe.

As the full impact of the message sank in, the assembly slowly began to sing the first verse of a familiar hymn.

"Now Thank We All Our God With Heart and Head and Voices...."

The words and melody brought everyone to their feet. Peter, Katya, Father, Mother and Aunt Lizzie rose with the others. Peter closed his eyes. The singing sounded better than in the days before the Revolution. There was more thanksgiving.

At the close of the hymn everyone left their seats and gathered round the stranger from North America asking for details about the food that was coming.

"It will be taken from the ship and carried by train to Halbstadt. Then you will bring a farm wagon and receive your share for Tiegen. The Soviet officials have given their permission. They will also be fed."

"Halbstadt." The Neufeld family called out the name together. There had been no word from Otto for over two years. If getting the food meant a journey to Halbstadt someone there might have a message from him; or someone might know of his whereabouts.

Peter knew differently. He wondered if he should break his vow and tell them — but he had promised Otto.

A local committee was formed at once to be in charge of the food distribution. The villagers voted without debate that Father would be the chairman. A food kitchen must be built at once in the school building, Mr. Hiebert said.

The hope of food gave strength even to those who were so weak they found it hard to walk to the meeting in the school. That afternoon the men and boys cemented a brick oven for the baking of bread. And before the day ended, a horse and carriage clattered down the village street with two large iron kettles.

"Enough to hold fifty gallons of soup," Aunt Lizzie announced, for she and Mother were to help with the cooking.

"The kitchen will feed over a thousand people each day,"

111

Father announced. "But there must be ration cards. We will feed the hungry of Tiegen and those who can come from the Russian countryside. Those with the greatest need will eat first."

While they waited for the supplies to arrive, those in the village who had been rationing small supplies of grain, offered to share all they had with those who had nothing.

Peter hammered a bench for the long tables where they would eat in the school. Katya sat patiently by his side and handed him nails. Hans Janzen helped them too.

For the first time in years, hope began stirring in Tiegen. Peter and Katya had grown, but in a tall, thin, fragile way. They didn't run or jump. They didn't have the strength. But they could sit at the table with the berry juice pens, and Peter taught Katya to read and write. There were drawings by Peter, too, one after another. Most of them were of open mouths and thin, drawn faces.

The famine years had kept the Neufelds close at home. For Peter the world had become as small as the rooms of their brick house, the barn, and the garden plot in their yard. Only when he read from the books stored by Teacher Enns in their cellar could he stretch beyond the walls and fences. And only when Father read aloud at night from the Bible did he feel a moment of peace and a small assurance of help.

With the arrival of Mr. Hiebert from North America, Peter felt suddenly that he could take a long deep breath again and walk beyond the garden, maybe even as far as the woods. Tiegen was no longer a forgotten village to be plundered. Russia was no longer separated from the rest of the world. The brown-haired man with the kind smile and the new suit had broken through the borders. The Mennonite brotherhood across the ocean was going to help them! Father said it was an answer to prayer.

One dark morning, with hopeful sprays of rain in the sky, Mishka and another half-starved horse were hitched to a farm wagon to go to Halbstadt for the first shipment of food. It was said there were sacks and sacks of white flour from Rosthern, Saskatchewan and Newton, Kansas.

"Such strange names," Peter said.

"Not strange at all," Aunt Lizzie said bluntly. "Those towns are filled with Mennonites who left our steppes many years ago."

No one argued with Aunt Lizzie.

Uncle Abram was chosen to drive the wagon to Halbstadt.

"Ask about Otto when you are there," Mother implored.

He promised.

The day before the wagon returned was lean and endless. Mother heated milk with tumbleweed seed and the warmth of it kept the Neufeld family alive.

Finally food arrived in the rattling farm wagon from Halbstadt. Boxes and bags of rice, barley, beans, fat, cocoa, wheat flour, and evaporated milk piled into the new Food Kitchen behind the freshly built oven and the smooth, scrubbed benches and tables. Wood and blocks of manure stood ready for burning beneath the kettles. It was a sight that brought tears to the eyes of mothers and fathers, for now their children would live.

A rolling can of evaporated milk fell from a box in the Food Kitchen and its wrappings dropped off. One one side was printed Honor Bound Milk. The other side was blank.

Peter lifted it from the ground. It could be used to write a letter to Otto. Through the years of the famine, Peter had written one letter after another to his brother and addressed it to the family in the Crimea. Each time he gave the letter to a traveller who came through the village, or a peasant who was on his way to the market of a city. He could not mail it in Tiegen, for the postman was his cousin and examined each piece of mail as though he was personally responsible for it.

But there had not been one reply. Peter wondered if Otto might be a prisoner once more, or lost in the vast land of the Crimea. Now he was determined to write again. This time he would ask the man from North America, Mr. Hiebert, to mail it. He would tell him why it had to be a secret.

113

When he returned with the food from Halbstadt, Uncle Abram brought one item of news about Otto that excited Father, Mother, and Aunt Lizzie.

"Otto was captured by the Red Army when the Self Defence disbanded," he told them, "but he escaped."

"Escaped!" they all cried together.

Peter had no comment. The news was two years old for him.

17

The centre of attention for Tiegen and the area surrounding it became the Food Kitchen. At noon when the hot meal was served lines of people gathered in front of it with their ration cards and their cups and bowls. Katya, Peter, Mother, and Aunt Lizzie had cards. They shared their portions with Father.

Mother and Aunt Lizzie helped bake the buns in the kitchen on the first day. Peter carried Katya's filled cup and bowl as well as his own to the table where Father waited.

Father prayed, but Peter didn't hear. His nose touched the top of the cup and he could feel the hot sweet liquid on his lips. But before he took one taste, he divided his portion with Father and helped lift Katya onto Father's knee.

She must not spill one drop of her food, they all agreed.

"It is warm and good," Katya laughed. "I can feel the cocoa running down into my feet."

Peter sipped his chocolate slowly. He wanted it to last forever. The bun was fresh and crunchy. The taste of the wheat in it was exactly like the wheat from the Ukraine. Katya fell asleep on Father's lap with a thick ring of chocolate around her lips.

"If only Esch could somehow have stayed alive," Peter said to Father. "The food from North America would have saved him."

In the days that followed rice was served, then beans, then cocoa again, and always with every meal were freshly baked buns.

Father's evening prayers were filled with thanksgiving, but he also prayed for Otto and Grandfather Penner.

Within a short time clothing arrived from Canada and the United States. More food came from the Mennonites in Holland. Drugs arrived for the doctors and the clinics. A tractor was sent to Tiegen with English lettering down the side of it. At last poor Mishka could stop pulling the plough and rest his half-starved body.

One day Mother gave Peter a large handful of wrappings from the Honor Bound Milk. A sparkle was in her eyes that Peter hadn't seen since the days before the Revolution.

"We won't tell Father about the paper, Peter," she laughed. "He tries, but he still doesn't understand about your wanting to draw pictures."

"I'll draw a picture of the Food Kitchen," Peter said excitedly.

To himself he decided that first he would make his letter to Otto longer and that he would finish it tomorrow. Mr. Hiebert had already promised to mail it in secret.

The next day a storm came with angry clouds that emptied rain in pools and streams over the dry earth. The drought was broken and the soaked roots in every garden sent up shoots of green. Peter heard talk among the men of rebuilding the village. Had the Red and White armies died of typhus and starvation? he wondered. Were the bandits all shovelled into one mass grave?

The high wind threatened the school building and the Food

Kitchen so Father with the other men gathered there to pound on extra boards and patch broken window panes. The women went along to protect the fires and cover the sacks of grain.

Katya, who had stayed at home with Peter, ran into the barn.

"Peter come," she cried, "an old man walked into the house."

"An old man, Katya?" Peter laughed. "You are telling me a story."

But she tugged and pulled him towards the house.

There was an old man inside. He was hunched and bent before the stove. His coat was shredded into tassles of rags, and his white hair hung like seaweed from a balding rock. A puddle of rain water settled at his feet and soaked through the cracks of his ancient boots. One shaking hand rested on a cane.

That white, blue-veined hand resting on a cane! Peter rushed towards the old man and looked into his face.

"Grandfather!" Peter threw his arms about the small, bent man.

Grandfather stared at his grandson. "You are strong and unharmed."

He drew Katya to him, "You have grown too. It is hard to believe."

In a jumble of words Peter told Grandfather about the Food Kitchens, the sacks of wheat and the new clothing from North America.

"There are a hundred and forty Food Kitchens in the villages of the Ukraine. Father says 40,000 people are being fed each day. Most of them are Mennonites, but many of the Russians eat with us too."

"Igor brought his old mother and his brothers and all their babies to eat in the kitchen," Katya added, proud that she knew as much to tell as Peter.

Grandfather sat by the fire in one of his favourite rocking chairs.

"I was expecting the worst," he smiled at both the children. "You are alive and the homestead is standing, even though mine is burned to the ground." He didn't seem surprised by this. Peter found dry straw for the fire, and placed a kettle of water on the cooking stove to heat.

"You must wash, Grandfather," Peter said. "I'll get you fresh clothes from the relief box that Father has brought home. Katya raced behind Peter, her short reddish braids bobbing up and down.

"Is there coffee, Peter?" Grandfather asked.

Katya jumped onto a chair and reached for a cup. She would make the coffee. She knew just how Mother did it.

The raging storm was forgotten and by the time it had calmed and the air was still and fresh Grandfather sat in his rocking chair by the stove, warmed and clean and sipping Katya's coffee. The young girl sat on his lap and Peter drew up a stool beside him.

When Mother, Father and Aunt Lizzie opened the hall door, they couldn't believe the scene before them.

"Father!" "Ezra!" the three of them cried out together. There seemed no need to know how he had come or from where. He was with them again. That was all that mattered.

A night of peace and calm filled the sky with low hanging stars and a thin new moon. Peter listened from his bed as the older people talked.

"I cannot talk of the prison," he heard Grandfather say. "It is a buried horror within me. With God's help, I survived. . . ."

"Yes I have heard about Otto. . . . The testing of his fatih was bitter. . . . Yes, I can forgive him for using a gun . . ."

Peter slept and then wakened again. Grandfather still talked.

"There is a lull in the efforts of the Soviet government now because of starvation and typhus — but their purpose has not changed. Our land will be government owned. The churches will remain closed. The schools will be run by the Soviets."

Peter listened carefully.

"Our Mennonite people can no longer live here and keep our faith." Grandfather's words now were firm and filled with conviction. "There is renewed talk of mass migration. . . . Thousands of Mennonites are signing petitions to ask for passports. . . . You must sign at once, Gerhardt, for every member of the family without delay."

117

Every muscle in Peter's body tensed. Grandfather was serious. They were going to move from the Neufeld homestead. They were going to leave Russia.

"But where can so many of us go?" Mother asked.

Grandfather clutched the handle of his cane. "There is already a colonization committee of Mennonites organized in Canada. The land is empty in the west. Farmers are needed there as they were needed once in the Ukraine. The newly elected Prime Minister, MacKenzie King, knows the Mennonites and wants us to come."

"But the land in the United States is large too," Father said.

"The government there has a quota and allows only a few immigrants to enter at a time. There are more than 20,000 Mennonites who want to migrate, Gerhardt!"

The number startled Peter.

"But will there be freedom in Canada?" Father asked. "Will there be conscription into the army? Can we build our own churches?"

"Yes, Gerhardt," Grandfather answered, "the offers are generous in this regard. But this time we will live among other Canadians. We must not withdraw from the native people as we have done in Russia."

Peter wondered how this would be possible.

"It is all very good, Father," Aunt Lizzie spoke out plainly, "but we have no money. Our homes and our lands are in ruins. Who will pay for thousands of us to cross the ocean and then ride in trains to the far west of Canada?"

Grandfather had an answer for this, too. "The Mennonites of North America are collecting money. One of their leaders, David Toews, has signed a contract with the Canadian Pacific Railway. They will grant credit for our passage if we farm and pay back our debts within five years.... Land is being bought along the railway on credit at very low rates."

Peter pressed his hands over his eyes. So much had happened while they were sick with typhus and then starving because of the drought and the Revolution. Peter had questions too. Who would live in the Neufeld homestead? Where would Otto go when he came home from the Crimea?

He was almost asleep when Grandfather jolted him totally awake.

"There is another grave problem for some of us," Grandfather said. "Those who emigrate must pass a medical examination by a Canadian doctor. I am old and ill and I could never pass the test."

The following morning Peter finished his long letter to Otto. He told him everything that had happened and ended it with:

> You must come home, Otto. Grandfather says he can't go to Canada with us because he is ill. Who will take care of him? I have decided to give him your address because I know he will keep it a secret.
> Your brother,
> Peter

Peter walked to the Food Kitchen and found Mr. Hiebert who promised to mail the letter that afternoon.

18

"Grandfather Penner is home!" Peter spread the news through all of Tiegen.

The weakened old man sat day after day rocking in his chair by the Neufeld stove. His cane steadied him as he leaned forward to listen and to talk, for he could no longer stand on his legs. The trials of prison had been too much for them. Peter became his constant companion.

"I have so much to do in Tiegen and there is so little time," he told all those who gathered around him. Neighbours and even distant friends came to him for counsel and advice. Questions filled the room.

"Shall we emigrate?"... "Shall we sell our homes?"... "We are exhausted in mind and in body, Grandfather, what shall we do?"... "How do we explain the Self Defence and our young men fighting the Red Army after 400 years of non-resistance?"

Grandfather listened with patience, and Peter marvelled that he always had answers.

"All who can must emigrate and start a new life in a country where there is freedom of religion," Grandfather told them. "Russia is no longer our Fatherland. Our petitions to Moscow seeking permission to rebuild our churches and our schools have been unanswered".... "Mennonite leaders from sixty villages have met and declared that they still believe in not resisting violence. What has happened with the Self Defence is unfortunate. We are sorry that we did it."

When they were alone, Peter asked Grandfather if he should write to Otto again.

"I have written to him," the old man confided to Peter. "I am certain that he is alive. But we must keep this secret between the two of us."

"But why hasn't he answered any of my letters, Grandfather?"

"I have decided it is too dangerous for him, Peter." Grandfather was thoughtful. "I am going to write to one of our church elders in the Crimea and have him talk with Otto."

One name after another was added to the long list of those who asked for passports to North America. Father wrote down each name in the Neufeld family. Aunt Lizzie added her name in large scrawling letters beneath them.

Surely Grandfather would sign the petition too. Peter wiped from his mind all thoughts of his useless legs and the doctor's examinations. Father could carry him onto the train and onto the ship. And Otto would surely come home in time to leave with them.

Homesteads were put up for sale to pay for the trip to Canada. Some were purchased by Russians who moved into the villages. Auctions were held.

Aunt Lizzie bristled when someone suggested that the silver tea urn would bring a good price: "I will sell my shoes before I will part with my samovar." From the torn, ragged blanket in which she wrapped it, she also uncovered the small silver and gold medallion with the Tsar's coat-of-arms moulded into one side. It was the one Uncle Herman had worn around his neck.

"I want Peter to have this when we get to the new country." Aunt Lizzie held the gold piece tenderly in the palm of her hand.

Grandfather examined the medallion closely.

"If you keep it, Lizzie, you had better hide it well," he said. "If a Soviet official found it on you, you would be shot."

"I know, Father." Aunt Lizzie was not alarmed. "Perhaps I am becoming like you, I no longer have any fear."

How could they not have fear? Peter was amazed. He was constantly afraid that the soldiers and the bandits might return or that the Soviet officials in the village would begin to enforce their stern rules again.

But it did seem to be a time of rest for the country to recover from the sickness of war and revolution. Part of Father's land was returned to him. Another tractor arrived from the Mennonites of North America to be used in Tiegen for spring planting. Not one horse was left with strength to pull a plough. The villagers marvelled at the great machine and its churning wheels that demanded no human muscle.

The school opened and the Mennonite children entered cautiously. Teacher Enns was there but only as an assistant. There were no courses in religion or in German and the teachers were Russians, approved by the Soviets. Peter felt big and awkward for the grade he was now in. After many years away from school, all the children were shy and ill at ease. There had been no time for them to be together during the days of famine and revolution. And now the school was not at all as they remembered it.

At the end of a class period, a Russian teacher spoke to Peter.

121

"You are a bright student, Peter Neufeld," he said. "I've heard that you are also an artist. Your people plan to leave our country and move to North America. Why?"

Peter didn't answer, but he was pleased by this special attention.

"If you go to North America," the teacher said briskly, "you will have to buy a car and earn money. They care only about making money in those countries. They have no interest in art."

"Thank you for telling me." Peter tipped his visor cap politely and walked quickly away. He asked Grandfather about this at once when he got home.

"You will always draw pictures, Peter, just as your Father will always sing. These are gifts from God. No one can take them from you."

The next day at school there was another statement from the teacher that Peter brought home. He spoke of it at the evening meal.

"Today at school," Peter announced, "the teacher said we do not need God because the government will give us bread. He said we don't have to pray because the old God is dead."

There was stark silence. Not a spoon was lifted. There was not even the sound of breathing.

Mother was the first to speak. "I have wanted to stay in our home in Tiegen. It grieves me to leave Grandfather behind. But, now I know that we must emigrate. Without God, Peter, our Mennonite people will perish."

That evening Father wrote a letter to Uncle Jacob in Nebraska who had sent the Indian suits for Christmas.

> We have not offended those in authority here. It is that we do not wish to and cannot leave religion. We can commit ourselves to communism; that is, we can share possessions with others and work communally. To join the circle of the ungodly, however, is beyond our ability — then we must flee, if possible.

On a hot summer morning the Canadian doctor arrived to examine all those with passports. He wore a stiff white coat, thin narrow pants, and polished brown leather shoes. He set up his office in a room at the school. The frightened villagers washed themselves and their tattered clothes as best they could. The doctor's table was scrubbed and the air about him was sterile.

The Neufelds with Aunt Lizzie stood one after the other in the line outside the doctor's office.

"No cripples will be examined," a nurse in an outer office announced.

Peter was shocked. Grandfather would not even be examined. How could he move half way across the earth and never see Grandfather again? And, there had still been no letter from Otto.

The doctor found many in the group who had trachoma, an infectious eye disease. They could not go. But the Neufelds and Aunt Lizzie were well and their passports were stamped. They rejoiced in silence.

Grandfather and Father seemed to concentrate all their time now on emigration. It was Peter who helped with the chores about the house and the barn and who planted the garden for those who would be left behind.

Each day a new announcement came.

"The Canadian Pacific Railway is sending ships for both credit and paying passengers. We must have people ready to fill them when they come!"

"750 Mennonites have emigrated from the old colony of Chortitza for Canada. They were the landless and the refugees. Mass migration is no longer a dream. It is happening!"

"We must leave soon, or the Soviet authorities will change their minds and no longer give us permission."

"The Canadian Pacific Railway has sent two long freight trains to take 1,000 emigrants from the station in Lichtenau. All who are going from Tiegen will leave then. The date is July 13. There is only one week left!"

A frenzy of packing followed this last announcement.

"I will take the silver samovar to Canada," Aunt Lizzie declared. "It, and the Tsar's medallion, is all I have from my home with Herman and our sons." She wrapped them in the tattered blanket.

Grandfather demanded that they pack his sixteen-volume encyclopedia. "There may be no schools at first. Peter will need them for his studies."

Boxes were built to hold the few linens and clothes that were left, and in the middle of one of them Mother tucked the green and gold-faced Prussian Kroeger clock that had hung on the wall of the big room since great-grandfather Neufeld built the homestead.

"I want to take my doll, Lizzie," Katya told all of them as she rocked with Grandfather in his chair. "And I need a suitcase that I can carry. I want to fill it with apples."

She remembers the apples we ate when the bandits came, Peter thought. They make her feel safe. That afternoon Peter built a small box with a handle and Katya filled it with red apples.

Father selected the best grain seeds to take to North America. Mother and Aunt Lizzie added apricot, cherry, apple and mulberry seeds. Aunt Lizzie wrapped up a small Russian olive shrub and seeds from the gooseberries and the watermelons. Father packed his German Bible and the Mennonite hymn book in the soft lining of his sheepskin coat.

Iron teakettles were left near the top of the boxes. They would be used on the long trip to boil water for tea. Mother patched black capes for herself and Aunt Lizzie. She stitched all the holes in Peter's and Father's loose britches and Katya's thick petticoats.

And in all the planning, the great worry about who would stay with Grandfather was solved. Teacher Enns came one evening and said, "I am staying to help in the school. I will watch over our Mennonite children who cannot migrate. I want to live with Grandfather Penner."

And the next day, Igor came to call.

"You cannot leave the Grandfather, who no longer has legs that walk, to live by himself. I will come with my old mother to cook and take care of the house and the barn."

19

Tension mounted in Tiegen as the day for departure came nearer. There was the apparent certainty of leaving and yet the nagging fear that the Soviets might change their minds overnight and cancel all the passports.

Peter and his friend Hans talked together about their excitement and their fears. They packed the Indian suits from Uncle Jacob in Nebraska far into the bottom of one of their baskets.

"We will see Indians in Canada," they whispered to one another.

The two of them with other men and boys of the village filled their farm wagons with tools and wood and travelled to Lichtenau. There they built strong double-deck bunk beds inside the cheaply made box cars that waited for them on the railroad tracks. They hammered together steps for the old people to enter the cars.

Father took charge. Forty people with all their luggage would travel together in each car. Father made a list and knew where everyone would stay.

At home, Mother, Aunt Lizzie and Katya baked boxes of zwieback to eat on the long journey.

Finally it was the last evening before the departure day. Supper was finished in the Neufeld home when Grandfather drew Peter beside his chair and suggested that they talk together while the others finished their packing.

"There is nothing I can do to help with my useless legs," Grandfather joked with the family, "but I never tire of talking. Perhaps you can spare Peter and let him listen to me."

The others were too busy to answer.

"Push my chair into the far corner, Peter, into the shadows."

Peter was puzzled, but obeyed.

"I want to talk with you about Otto." Grandfather lowered his voice to a whisper.

Peter's heart thumped as if a hammer was being pounded against it.

"Listen carefully to everything I say and don't attract the attention of the others."

Peter moved a stool close to the old man's chair.

"I have been writing to Otto and to Uncle Jacob in Nebraska," Grandfather said. "If Otto can escape across the Russian border and get to Holland, he can buy a ticket to the United States. Uncle Jacob will give him work and a home on his Nebraska farm."

"Why can't he come with us?" Peter still wanted Otto as well as Grandfather to go with their family on the Lichtenau train.

"He is still being hunted by the police. He would never be given a Russian passport."

Aunt Lizzie started towards them, then changed her mind and began packing more zwieback into a basket.

"Otto will need the rest of the money that was hidden in the stove," Grandfather continued, "to pay for transportation across the ocean."

"*Was* hidden?" Peter asked.

"Yes. Igor helped me take it from under the bricks last night and we've put the bills inside my leather belt."

"How can you get the belt to Otto? Where is he?" In his excitement Peter raised his voice. Grandfather grabbed his hand and steadied him.

"He is still disguised as a poor Ukranian peasant and he is on his way now to the border. Igor has given him the names of peasant friends along the way who will help."

"But the money..."

Grandfather interrupted. "You will take the money, Peter.

126

You will wear the belt around your shirt. It will be my farewell gift to you."

Peter's heart pounded faster.

"You will be searched by the Soviet soldiers before you cross the border. They will seize only jewels and large amounts of money. It's unlikely that a young boy's belt would attract attention. Be brave and calm, Peter, and I will pray for you."

Peter swallowed hard. He would do the best he could.

"When you arrive at the station in Riga, Latvia, before you get on the boat, one of the Mennonite leaders, who will meet the emigrants, is Fritz Claassen, a Dutch Mennonite. He is 6 feet 5 inches tall with thick blond hair. No one will be taller. Take the money from the belt and give it to him. He knows about Otto and he will see that he gets the money."

Peter sighed. "Then can I tell Father and Mother about Otto?"

Grandfather was thoughtful. "They will have so many worries, Peter. Wait until you know that Otto is safe in America. Then you can tell them."

"I wish you were coming with us." The closeness of Grandfather now and the permanent separation tomorrow seemed a cruel injustice. Grandfather's blue-veined hand gripped the handle of his cane.

"I'm an old man, Peter. My body would be bruised and beaten in the box cars and then again on the ship. But my mind and my spirit rejoice that you and Otto and the others are going to the free countries of North America. Only in such countries can our Mennonite faith flourish and grow. Free countries allow for differences among their people."

"But why did the bandits and the soldiers have to destroy Tiegen, Grandfather?" The anger against them had never quieted inside Peter. If they hadn't come, the village street would still be wide and clean swept, the orchards would be tended and bearing fruit, and the fields would soon be golden with grain for all of Russia. The church would be open and Grandfather would be preaching in it. He would be going to school. There was so much to learn. Peter wanted to cry out for the village and its good life that had disappeared.

Grandfather's head slowly nodded. The expression in his eyes was now that of a wise old man.

"I have lived all my life in the Ukraine of Russia, Peter, and I love this country. But there was great misery and suffering and poverty in this land. We Mennonites lived too much apart and didn't know."

"Why didn't the government change this?" Peter was finally asking the questions that had knotted and twisted inside him for days and months and years.. "Why did everyone start killing and stealing?"

"I have learned now, Peter, that the government of the Tsar was corrupt. The leaders thought only of themselves and their own family and friends. Otto warned us of a revolution and we Mennonites were caught unaware in the middle of it."

There was silence between the two of them for several minutes.

One question remained and Peter had to ask it.

"What about the Self Defence, Grandfather? Was it wrong for Otto and his friends to try and protect us?"

"I can't judge Otto and his friends, Peter." Grandfather leaned back in his chair exhausted. "I don't know what I would have done as a young man if I had seen all of my family treated brutally. But God has commanded us not to kill one another. When men begin to kill they can become brutes or they may forever be scarred as human beings."

"Then the Self Defence was wrong, wasn't it?" Peter answered the question himself.

"Yes it was wrong," Grandfather said, "and Otto believes this now too."

There was little sleep that night in the Neufeld farm home, and it was early dawn when Igor drove the farm wagon to the side door.

"The cherries are ripe on the orchard tree," Katya cried as the family began piling boxes and baskets into the straw-cushioned wagon. She ran to the tree and picked a handful and added them to the apples in her wooden case.

It was time to leave.

Grandfather sat quietly in his chair. Mother knelt beside him and kissed his cheek. She pressed a handkerchief over her mouth and ran towards the wagon.

Aunt Lizzie kissed him too, but looked into his face without a tear. "Each of us suffers differently, Father," she said. "You have given all of us courage. Bless you." She walked slowly to the buggy without looking back.

Father held Grandfather's hand. All the years of his life had been shared with Ezra Penner. There was no way to say goodbye.

Little Katya stood solemnly in front of them. Her red-gold braids shone like sparkling dew at the beginning a new day.

"I kissed Mishka goodbye." Tears began to run down her cheeks. "I told him you would take care of him, Grandfather. You won't forget, will you?"

"I won't forget, Katya." Grandfather smiled.

Igor came from the wagon. He made no effort to hide his tears. They ran over his black bearded face and onto his orange peasant shirt. He lifted Katya into his arms and carried her to the waiting wagon.

Peter waited at the back of the room.

"Here is my belt, Peter." Grandfather was excited. "Give your old one to me and put the new one on."

Peter quickly fastened the new belt around his waist.

"Now go, my boy." Grandfather pointed his cane towards the door. "Or the family will ride off without you."

20

When the Neufelds arrived at the station in Lichtenau, hundreds of buggies, carts, horses and people were already waiting beside the long lines of box cars.

Father and his helpers called out the family names and told everyone where to go. The Neufelds with Aunt Lizzie climbed into their car and shoved their baskets and boxes under the newly made bunk beds.

A shower of sparks belched from the smoke stack of the engine and the train wheels creaked and rolled.

A chorus of singing rose from the departing emigrants as the train slowly pulled away from the station: "Nun ade du mein lieb Heimatland" "Now Farewell my Beloved Homeland," the people sang as they waved to the familiar faces of lifelong friends and relatives who were left behind.

There was no laughter among the people in the boxcars. Aunt Lizzie held the ragged blanket with the silver samovar and the silver and gold-decorated medallion on her lap, sitting cross-legged on the straw-covered floor. She looked pale and thin and frequently coughed. She squeezed Mother's hand. "I feel as though something has been torn from my body."

Mother watched anxiously for Father who still ran along the station platform, closing doors and checking that no one had been left behind. Peter sat on a top bunk with his long legs dangling in the air. He held onto the new belt with both hands and vowed not to take it off until he got to Riga. Katya was beside him. Her chubby arms clutched her doll and wooden suitcase with the apples and cherries from the Neufeld orchard.

At last Father swung himself into the car and half closed the sliding door. The wide thickness of his body pushed everyone backwards.

"Poppa is too big for this little car." Katya's small clear voice rose above the clattering train wheels. The children in the car laughed and even Father smiled. The train began to speed up and the wheels clicked faster and faster.

An hour later the train entered a Russian village and the brakes screeched to a stop. Ill-clad, hungry Russian peasants clustered around their car.

"Give us food," they begged. "We will give you dishes and pieces of cloth."

"How I understand their suffering." Mother watched them with compassion. "Without the Food Kitchens we would still be starving." But she guarded the box of toasted zwieback. They needed all of them for their long journey.

Peter grabbed the iron teakettle and jumped with Katya from the bed. Others were running along the station platform to fill their kettles from the boiling water pot at the station.

"A cup of hot Russian tea is what I need," Aunt Lizzie coughed and huddled over her blanket.

"Don't get sick, Lizzie." Mother glanced at her anxiously.

They had to stay well. Peter knew this for when they crossed the Russian border into Riga, Latvia there would be another medical check. Those who passed this final test would board the great ship that was waiting for them at the dock in Riga. Those who were sick would be taken to a refugee camp in Lechfeld, Germany. It was impossible for emigrants to remain with a sick relative. The cost would be too great for the Board of Colonization.

The train whistle blew and passengers ran for their cars. Father saw that every head was counted before waving the signal to start.

As Peter lifted Katya to the top bunk he noticed that her cheeks were flushed. He pressed his hand over her head. It was hot and dry.

"If she sleeps she will be better," he argued with himself. "I won't worry Mother." Peter leaned her head against his shoulder. He could feel the fever through his heavy coat sleeve.

But Peter's main alarm and fear throughout the next day were for himself. Father had said very little about the search that would take place before they travelled through the Red Gate across the Russian border. Perhaps he thought there were no valuable items left among the emigrants. He and Father had already agreed that Katya's doll would be left under a blanket on the lower bunk bed when the search took place.

Peter tried to think about Otto and where he would cross the border. It would be at night. There would be barbed wire. He might have to swim across a river naked with his clothes tied on the top of his head. He could easily be shot or captured. But even these terrifying thoughts didn't take his mind off the belt. It burned around his waist like a ring of flaming straw. If the soldiers started to take the belt from him, he would grab it and run, he decided.

Peter's mind was so filled with fear of the search, that he didn't notice that the train was slowing down. It jerked and then stopped. Both Peter and Katya fell to the floor.

The door of the box car jerked open abruptly. Peter wasn't prepared for the sudden entrance of four Russian soldiers, two men and two women. Their eyes stared straight ahead of them with no flicker of expression.

Can they even see us? Peter wondered, clutching his belt with both hands in sharp panic. The same cold terror that had knotted his stomach into a ball of ice in the days and nights of the Revolution, seized him. Katya was suddenly beside him, clutching his leg and muffling her sobs against the coarse patches of his trousers. He put one arm around her.

"Form two lines to be searched," one of the soldiers ordered in Russian. "The men on one side and the women on the other."

Katya didn't move, and Peter held her tight against him.

The soldiers started at either end of the lines. Peter and Katya and the other children were in the middle. Peter watched the soldiers' searching hands slide over shirts and trousers, turn out pockets, shake caps inside out, and fold back sleeves.

For some reason the nearest soldier paid no attention to Katya. He didn't touch her. But then it was Peter's turn. The ball of ice in his stomach began to make him sick and the soldier in front of him seemed to be spinning around and around at a dizzy pace. Peter thought he might fall to the floor, so he closed his eyes. He could feel hands pressing against his chest, then under his arms. They moved closer to the belt. A long finger slid under it around his stomach and then against his back. Another finger rubbed over the top of the belt.

"Take off your shoes," the soldier shouted close to Peter's face. Peter's eyes opened and the spinning stopped. It looked as if the soldier was not going to take off his belt.

Father was already barefoot.

The baskets and boxes were being opened and searched. Aunt Lizzie held the tattered blanket that covered her samovar, and Mother stood close beside her.

"Why do you carry a worn-out blanket, old grandmother?" a woman soldier shouted at Aunt Lizzie.

Aunt Lizzie twisted the blanket more tightly around the samovar and as she did so Peter noticed the medallion fall to the floor.

He quickly picked it up.

"What's that?" the woman soldier shouted.

Peter held it out to her in the open palm of his hand, and as he did he remembered Grandfather's words: "You could be shot for carrying a gift from the Tsar."

The woman soldier barely looked at it. Peter glanced up at her in surprise. She wore thick glasses. She couldn't see the Tsar's coat of arms on the upward side of the oval silver and gold medal.

"Stupid boy," she said, "give it back to the old grandmother."

At long last the search ended and the sliding door of the box car banged shut. But it didn't lock and as the train started up it began to slide open.

"We are nearing the Red Gate," Father said quietly in low German.

Peter looked outside. Clusters of soldiers were grouped along

133

the tracks and just ahead of them was a tall steel frame shaped like a barn. A big star stuck to the top of it, and high above, on something that looked like a ladder leading into the sky, was the Red Flag of the Soviets flapping against a hot orange sky.

The train jerked as though it were stopping again. Peter saw Mother and Aunt Lizzie bow their heads in earnest prayer. Peter prayed, too, but his eyes were wide open. Katya's head was still buried into the cloth of his trousers. He could feel the heat from her fever against his leg, but it seemed of little importance compared to the urgent need for the train to keep moving. Father's strong body leaned against the box-car wall as though trying to push it forward.

But the train didn't stop. It creaked slowly and steadily ahead, and then Peter saw the steel frame of the Red Gate opposite the open door. The train passed through and they were on the other side of the border!

Peter lifted Katya into the air. Her cheeks were red and flushed, but she smiled down at him knowing without asking that something good had happened.

"We'll never see the Soviet soldiers again," Peter called up to her.

The train screeched and stopped finally beside an open field of tall grass and thin stemmed yellow flowers.

A tumult rolled from the box cars in cascades of laughter and shouted prayers. The quiet, simple emigrants from Tiegen felt the weight and oppression of the Revolution lift from their hearts. "Now Thank We All Our God...," they sang, as they had when Mr. Hiebert had come to the Ukraine with the food from North America. Peter pulled the money belt from his waist and waved it in the air.

The tall grass of a new land blew about their feet and the family knelt to the ground as Father read from his Bible a Psalm of thanksgiving.

21

Slowly they walked back to the box cars, but the doors stayed open as the wheels of the train began to roll. There was no longer any need to hide. Soon they would see the station in Riga, Latvia.

Not long after Father called out, "We are in Riga!"

Mother tied her shawl about her head and, standing up, reached for Katya on the top bunk. She cried out in alarm. Katya's face and neck were covered with red patches.

"Katya has the measles!"

Father didn't hear. The train stopped and the passengers lined up for inspection in a large building nearby. Aunt Lizzie coughed hoarsely and pulled her black shawl around her shoulders.

Father joined them. He was alarmed when he saw Katya.

"Measles," he said at once.

They joined the long line of emigrants who seemed to be walking swiftly through the examination hall. Peter lagged behind. He must find the tall man from Holland. He had already taken the money from his belt and had the bills folded in his pocket. But no one stood high above the others in the crowd.

The tired impatient doctor examined each of them quickly.

"The mother, father and son are well," he said. "But the little girl has the measles. She cannot go to Canada. Also the old lady there." He pointed to Aunt Lizzie. Her loose face was haggard and pale. "She needs rest and medication. She does not have my permission to go either."

He waved his hands impatiently for them to leave and another official person stepped forward saying that Katya and Aunt Lizzie must get their baggage at once and go with him to the detention camp in Lechfeld, Germany.

The shock was great.

"But my little girl is so ill," Mother cried.

Father knelt beside her and chose his words carefully.

"There are a thousand emigrants in this building who must soon board the ship for Canada, Marie," he said gently to Mother. "Lizzie will care for Katya as well as any of us. We must be thankful that she can stay with her."

He leaned over Katya and kissed her forehead.

Then he turned to Peter.

"Uncle Abram and I must meet with the ship's officers at once. You will have to take my place with the family, Peter."

Peter was torn. He must look for the tall Mr. Claassen, but he must also help Mother. Father started to walk away and then returned quickly with a hurried request.

"Tell Aunt Lizzie about the doll. They will need the money at the detention camp.

Mother was too bewildered and shaken to know what they were saying.

Peter sat beside his aunt. He told her quickly about the money they had stuffed inside Katya's doll.

"We will need the money," said Aunt Lizzie calmly. "This delay will add to the expense of our trip." She put her lean, firm hand on Peter's arm.

"Don't worry about your little sister, Peter. No task, it seems, is too hard for me. But I worrry about your Mother. She was always fragile and sensitive and trusted everyone. It's a wonder that she has survived the Revolution."

Peter went to Katya and Mother. Already his sister was crying as Mother was trying to explain what was going to happen. Peter picked up the small wooden case filled with apples.

"Katya, listen to me."

Katya looked at him with feverish, tear-filled eyes.

"You will get better. I had measles once and look how big and strong I am. Aunt Lizzie will take care of you and when you are well you will both come to Canada on another ship."

Peter opened the small wooden suitcase. He counted the apples with Katya. There were ten of them.

"When you get on the ship to come to Canada," Peter told her, "eat one apple every day. When you eat the last apple you will be with all of us in Canada."

Katya counted the apples again. "Ten days?" she said. She could understand the time of separation now and her arms reached out for Aunt Lizzie.

"But don't start counting until you get on the ship," Peter warned.

The parting came so suddenly that the emptiness was like the sudden disappearance of a falling star from the sky on a dark summer night.

"Katya and Aunt Lizzie will join us soon," Peter said to Mother, trying to convince himself that this was true.

Mother's friend Lydia joined her. Peter slipped away from them. He began to search frantically through the crowds for a tall man with thick blond hair.

"I'll have to tell Father," Peter decided, when a hand grabbed him on the shoulder. He spun around. A ragged beggar stood behind him with a heavy beard and uncombed hair. His hands were scratched and bleeding. But his eyes were alive with happiness.

"Otto!" Peter grabbed his brother's hand.

Relief and joy bound them together for a brief reunion.

"I am still in great danger, Peter." Otto lowered his head. "I could be arrested and returned to Russia for I have no official papers. You must not tell Mother and Father that you have seen me."

Peter quickly handed his brother the folded money.

Otto stuffed it inside his shirt.

"The money means a new life for me, Peter. How can I ever thank you and Grandfather enough? Someday I will repay all of it."

"But you are so ragged and thin, Otto." Peter felt helpless. "What can I do for you now?"

"We must think only ahead, Peter." Otto searched through the crowds hoping for a glimpse of Father, Mother, Katya or Aunt Lizzie. Peter decided not to alarm him with the news of the illness and separation.

"The tall man, Mr. Claassen, couldn't come to the station, but I will meet him soon and go to Holland."

"But Otto, where will I see you again?"

"In North America!" Otto tossed his head with his old buoyancy. "They say the boundary between the United States and Canada is peaceful and without guards. We will see each other often." Otto turned quickly and disappeared into the crowd.

22

Peter hardly noticed the ship in Riga harbour. His thoughts were on Katya and Aunt Lizzie in the detention camp, and on ragged Otto trying to get to Holland. Where in Germany was Lechfeld? How far was it from Holland? Peter tried to remember the maps of Europe in his Russian geography book.

He held onto Mother, who was pale and silent, as they stepped onto the ship. The floor beneath them dipped up and down. How could one ship hold a thousand people with all their boxes and baskets?

The ship began to ease away from the shore. A sudden homesickness swept over Peter, for the great ocean ahead seemed a more final separation than the long stretches of land that had taken them so far away from the Ukraine.

Mother and Peter stood at the ship's rail until all sight of land had disappeared.

"I hope, Peter, that I am strong enough for this journey," Mother sighed.

Peter noticed for the first time how small and how fragile she was. He remembered Aunt Lizzie's final words to him. He would have to take care of her since Father was so busy.

Many hours later, their ship slipped into another port called Antwerp. Here the emigrants boarded a steamship so huge Peter wondered if it might be a separate country floating on the water.

"It's the Canadian Pacific Railway steamship the *Minnedosa*," Hans Janzen called to Peter. "Let's board it together and wave goodbye from the highest deck!"

But Father and Uncle Abram directed all of them into the bottom of the ship. Families were separated into rooms with rows of bunk beds more closely packed together than the box car beds in the Russian train. Round windows gave a blue, dim light.

"We're under the sea!" Peter realized, watching the bubbles of water spray against the glass. At long last excitement for the trip began slowly to capture Peter's interest. Hans tugged at his arm, pleading with him to climb to the upper deck.

"Alright," Father said when the boys looked towards him, "but come back soon."

Together they climbed spirals of steps until the fresh sea air blew at their visor hats and billowed the wideness of their home-made pants. When they reached the highest deck, they looked down and the distance to the water below made Peter feel that he was falling overboard. He clung to the rail and grabbed Hans's hand.

Steam from the giant funnels exploded into the air with whistles shrieking; and the massive floating city pulled away from the shore. A man in slim pants with a bright plaid coat took the straw hat from his head and threw it far out to sea. A friend beside him cheered his gesture of farewell.

Peter was captivated by this. To leave one land and sail across the Atlantic to another certainly demanded some kind of ceremony. He took his own Russian visor cap and gave it a swing into the air that carried it up into the sky and so far out to sea that it was a dot on the water when it landed.

Hans stood open-mouthed.

"It's your only cap, Peter. What will your father say?"

"It's a Russian cap, Hans," Peter shouted above the whistling steam. "We're going to a new country. I'll get another cap in Canada."

The reason for the missing cap remained a secret between them. Father and Mother were displeased with Peter's loss. Clothing was scarce among them and carefully guarded.

The excitement of the departure celebration was brief. The bunks in the bottom of the ship were filled with seasick passengers, and Mother, pale and thin, looked at Peter without recognition. Then Peter himself became ill.

"You are both still weak from the typhus," he heard Father say.

Memories floated through Peter's mind. He was standing again in the Neufeld brick home in Tiegen with drunken soldiers sprawled over their chairs and aiming their guns at Father, Mother, and Aunt Lizzie. He could smell the filth and sickness of the typhus plague and then the ache of the horrible hunger that drew their cheeks against their bones. He could hear Katya crying out and clinging to his arm. Would these memories always be inside him?

After a few days they felt somewhat better. They climbed the stairs to the upper deck for fresh air. They were surprised to find Uncle Abram standing by the rail talking and laughing with a white-haired Jewish grandfather whose head was circled by a small black skull cap. Abram bid his new friend goodbye and joined them.

"That fine old man is also a refugee from the Soviets," he said.

"And when did you learn to speak Hebrew, Abram?"

Mother was amazed.

Uncle Abram laughed again. "He speaks Yiddish and I speak low German and we understand one another."

"That would be something to hear." Mother and Peter joined in the laughter.

When they returned to their cabin again, Mother found a clean tablet of paper in a trash bin and some pencils in a deep corner of their basket.

"Draw pictures to send to Katya, Aunt Lizzie, and Grandfather," she suggested to Peter.

Peter smoothed a place on his bed and leaned back against the ship's wall. The room no longer seemed like a dark, cramped tunnel. Peter began to draw pictures of the ship with its high rails and watery portholes. He sketched the ocean and the arched-winged seagulls that flapped along behind them.

Mother watched eagerly. "When we get to the new country, you must study to be an artist."

"An artist, Mother?" Peter was surprised. He looked at her closely, and saw that she really meant it.

On the ninth day at sea land was sighted.

"It's the tip of Nova Scotia in Canada." Father told Peter and Mother when they joined him on the top deck.

There was a hushed silence among the watching immigrants. Land took clearer shape and finally there was land on every side of them.

Next morning the ship would dock in the province of Quebec, Father said.

Peter thought of the great stork that glided onto its nest on the high roof of the Penner barn at home. Their ship was like the stork, folding its wings for a landing after a long flight.

"We are the second shipload of Russian Mennonites to arrive," Peter heard Father say as they walked off the ship in Quebec with their baskets and boxes and into a barn-like Immigration Hall. "The Canadian Pacific Railway and the Mennonite Colonization Board have agreed to settle 20,000 of us in this new country."

141

"Twenty thousand!" Mother exclaimed.

Inside the building, announcements were being made in German about where each family would go. "The Mennonites of Ontario are offering temporary homes for 875 of the passengers," Peter heard. The Neufelds would go there and then later travel west to seek a farm.

The places meant nothing to Mother and Peter, but Father seemed disappointed. He had heard of the province of Manitoba where the prairie land was like the steppes of the Ukraine.

"We will go there later," Mother assured him. "Perhaps it is easier for Katya and Aunt Lizzie to come to Ontario," Father said. He had left them earlier to seek more information. "The Mennonites in Ontario came from Pennsylvania in the United States. Some of their ways of living are different from ours but their beliefs are the same."

Peter and Hans sat together with their faces flat against the train window. At first they saw only rocks and forests and small blue lakes. Could this be the land in Canada where grain could be planted? Uncle Abram shook his head.

They passed small strips of farms.

"Look at the little pieces of barns." Father was worried. "Where do they keep their crops?"

The train travelled on and the farms became larger and the land flattened into fields. The passengers began to relax.

The trip stretched into hours and then through the night. It was morning when a trainman announced,

"The next stop is Erb Street, Waterloo."

"This is where we get off." The words spread up and down the train car among the rustle of boxes and baskets that were shoved and lifted.

Mother smoothed the wrinkles from her long skirt and tied the black shawl more tightly around her head. Father moved to the front of the train car. Peter wondered if he should have kept his Russian cap after all, for Hans clamped his down over his head as though it were a shield and a protector.

"I wish Katya and Aunt Lizzie and Otto and Grandfather were with us." Mother spoke aloud the wish that had been on Peter's mind ever since they arrived in Canada.

23

Stepping off the train in Waterloo became a dream to Peter. Along both sides of the city street were rows of buggies, cars and people. They gathered around the newly arrived Russian Mennonites, speaking English words and a strange German they called "Pennsylvania Dutch."

The boys of Peter's age tucked their shirts inside their pants. Peter's shirt hung out like the peasants of the Ukraine with grandfather's belt around it.

Father, in his Russian visor hat, stood on a farm wagon and motioned for everyone to listen. Could they understand him, Peter wondered? He spoke in high German. He gave thanks to God for their safe arrival and then called the new country a place of freedom, opportunity, and new hope.

Mother clung to Peter's arm. They began walking down the middle of the street. Somehow the boxes and baskets trailed behind them in carts and buggies. Peter thought of the invading armies walking down the wide street of Tiegen.

"We are invading," he whispered to Mother, "but we aren't an army."

Mother laughed.

A sturdy brick church loomed before them, and all the newly arrived immigrants turned into it as though into their own home. Smells of coffee and food drifted from its doors. They were a warmer welcome than the strange new languages. There were plates of delicious cut-up white bread with cheese and meat between them. "Sandwiches," Peter heard them called.

Father and Uncle Abram bent their heads to talk with the ministers of the church. The people of Waterloo were expecting 600 people and now there were 875. New homes had to be found. Some people took twelve immigrants instead of two.

It turned out that Father, Mother and Peter would go with a Mr. and Mrs. Weber to their country home in their black buggy; Hans and his family would live in the town; Uncle Abram would go to a place called Baden. At last everyone had a home.

"How can they be so good to us?" Mother spoke with awe. "We are complete strangers to them."

Mother asked that their letters be mailed with Peter's drawings inside. She asked if a letter had come from the detention camp in Germany. No, there were no letters.

Peter spoke out boldly asking about a letter from Uncle Jacob in Nebraska.

"And why would you hear from Uncle Jacob?" Father wanted to know. Peter almost told him, wondering how much longer he must keep Otto's secret.

Morning slid into afternoon and then into evening and the dream continued for Peter. It was getting dark and inside the church bright electric lights blinked on. Lights appeared on top of poles along the street. Lights on the cars made round balls of racing fire. Lights twinkled like showers of stars along a shopping street not far away. There had not been one electric light in all of Tiegen.

If Katya were here she would clap her hands and Aunt Lizzie's wide smile would spread across her face. Peter yearned for them.

Father, Mother and Peter rode into the night with the kindly Webers until they came to a farm house with a kerosene lantern in the window.

"You will live in our 'Grossdoddy House' for a while." They opened the door of a little house attached to their bigger one.

"Our Grandfather died and it is empty until we are old enough to live in it," they explained.

"We will not unpack our boxes until Katya and Aunt Lizzie come," said Mother. "Tomorrow we may have another home."

But Father closed the door of this first home in Canada and drew them close together as he read from his Bible and prayed for those who were missing.

Peter's dream had not ended for the day — for the Webers called them to supper. "A feast great enough for the Tsar," exclaimed Father as they ate thick slices of beef, green beans from the garden, hot gravy on potatoes, slices of pie, and dishes of canned strawberries.

When the next day came it was still a dream. Some of the immigrants were being offered jobs in the Rubber Factory in town. Would Father like such a job?

"How can I say no?" Father looked desperate and miserable. "We need the money to pay the railway for our travel debt."

"Gerhardt is a farmer." Mother spoke out for him. She has a new courage to go with a new country, thought Peter. He was proud of her.

So Father became the hired man for Mr. Weber. He saved each penny of his small wages to pay the travel debt. Peter milked the cow. Mother baked zwieback and pulled weeds in the garden.

Day after day there was no mail in the box that stood on top of a pole near the road. Then Mrs. Weber explained that it came only once each week, when someone from town delivered it all at one time.

But two weeks passed and still there were no letters. Mother cried in the night when she thought the others were asleep. Peter could hear her.

At the end of four weeks, three letters came all at once. The letter from Germany was opened first. Mother tore apart the envelope with trembling fingers.

This is to inform you that your daughter Katya is well again and will be able to come on the next ship of emigrants from Russia. You may expect her at the railway station in

Kitchener, Ontario, on August 20. She will have her name and address pinned to the sleeve of her dress. Her aunt, Mrs. Herman Klassen (Lizzie) died quietly last night. We will bury her here and a Mennonite minister in the camp will conduct the service. Your daughter, Katya, knows about the death.

"Lizzie dead!" Mother steadied herself by holding Father's arm.

"Strong, courageous Aunt Lizzie," Peter said. His heart ached for her.

"She waited to die until she thought we could get along without her," Father said thoughtfully. "She will never know how much we still need her. . . . But Katya is coming." He almost sang the words.

"Katya will be here in a week." Mother checked off the days on the wall calendar. "She will be travelling alone and she is only seven."

The second letter was from a distant cousin, Cornelius Dyck in Steinback, Manitoba.

We got your address from the Colonization Board. We are thankful that you are safe and in North America. You must come to Manitoba. It is possible for you to purchase a farm on credit with another immigrant family. The work will be hard, but you can do it. Come at once.

Father's face looked as if the sun had settled on it. He could work to own his own farm again. He could live in a country with wide, flat land like the steppes of Southern Russia.

"Shall we go?" he asked Mother and Peter.

They smiled. How could they say no?

The third letter was addressed just to Peter, but all of them could see that it was from Uncle Jacob in Nebraska.

"I must read it alone," Peter said solemnly.

The letter contained bad news. Peter was shocked. Uncle Jacob had not seen or heard from Otto since Grandfather's letter arrived the day the Neufelds left Russia. Otto must have been captured. Perhaps the money in the belt had been stolen. Peter had been so certain that they would see each other in North America. He tucked the letter under his shirt.

"It's a secret from Uncle Jacob that I can't tell you yet," he said to his parents. He wanted desperately to tell Father and Mother, but he remembered Grandfather's words: "Wait until you know that Otto is safely in America, then you can tell your parents." He would have to wait.

The kindly Webers arranged a memorial service for Aunt Lizzie in their country church. Many of the newly arrived immigrants with their Waterloo County hosts and hostesses came to sorrow. Uncle Abram and Hans Janzen and his family were among those who talked with Peter.

Later at home in their "Grossdoddy House," the Neufelds began making plans for Katya's arrival. And Father wrote a letter to Cousin Cornelius. They would come to Manitoba as soon as Katya arrived.

On the morning of August 20, the Neufelds borrowed the black buggy from the Webers to make the trip to the railway station in Kitchener. Mother sat forward in the buggy seat urging Father to go faster. Father whipped the horse into a near gallop.

When they arrived at the station it was filled with relatives and friends. Even the Webers had borrowed another buggy to be there. Father spread his arms wide apart as though to embrace the Webers and everyone who had helped them.

"Thank you for sharing our joy as well as our sorrow," he said.

A whistle sounded far down the tracks. Bells began to ring. Would Katya really be on this train? Would she know how to get off alone at this station? The engine came near and braked itself to a stop. A train conductor jumped from a door with some steps which he placed on the station platform. Two men with new baggage walked down them. They were followed by a fat lady with her little boy.

Where was Katya?

Then a little girl appeared. She carried a small wooden suitcase and a large doll with a china face.

"Katya!" Mother, Father, and Peter called out her name together.

She looked at them shyly. Her red-gold braids hung long and thick over her shoulders. She was taller and her cheeks were not as round.

"Does she know us?" Peter asked softly, for none of them moved.

The train porter carried a large box and placed it at her feet.

"It's Aunt Lizzie's samovar," Mother whispered. "She sent it with Katya."

Katya put her suitcase on the platform and opened it. She pulled out a small red apple, walked up to Peter and took a bite from it looking straight at him.

"Aunt Lizzie put ten apples inside," she said to him, "but I had to wait two days to eat the last one so I would get here like you said, Peter."

Laughing, Peter lifted his sister into his arms. Katya threw her arms around his neck. Then it was Mother's turn to hug her, and at last Father reached for her with his big strong hands. Katya smiled at them happily. She waved to Uncle Abram and called out to Hans Janzen and his family.

"On the ship there was a woman who held me up to the round window just like Peter's picture," she said. They all laughed with joy and relief.

The paper that read "Katya Neufeld, Kitchener, Ontario, Canada" was pinned to the sleeve of her dress as the letter had said. Father took it off and stuffed it into his pocket.

Father was ready to flick the reins to start when Katya said soberly, "Aunt Lizzie died."

"Yes we know, Katya. We got a letter telling us about it," Mother said.

Katya didn't cry.

"Aunt Lizzie told me that she was tired and she was ready for the Lord to take her," Katya said simply.

"I think that was true," Father answered, as he drove the buggy slowly into the country.

24

The Neufelds left for Steinbach, Manitoba the day after Katya arrived. Again there was an outpouring of friends and relatives at the railway station to wish them safety and God's blessings.

Katya, who had been a shy, quiet little girl during the terrors of the Revolution, chattered constantly. Most of the time she talked about Aunt Lizzie.

"I sat in her hospital room every day," she told her family. "We laughed and laughed about when Aunt Lizzie was a little girl in Grandfather's big house in Tiegen. Once she climbed to the top of the apple tree and couldn't get down. Grandfather had to get a big ladder and go up after her."

"I remember," Mother smiled.

Peter thought about what Aunt Lizzie had said when she was suffering from the shock of Uncle Herman's murder: "A child must have laughter to grow." She had given Katya laughter.

The Webers prepared food for the Neufelds to take on their trip. The time had been short with them. But they had opened the door of welcome for Father, Mother and Peter and each one of them felt a special gratitude.

When the train pulled away from the Kitchener station, the Neufelds were the only immigrant family in the car. They sat together in their black shawls and home-made Russian clothes. There was no fear or shyness in their manner. They were going together to a new home in North America.

They watched the changing landscape through the window of the flying train. In the strange looking bundles and boxes around their feet were the treasured seeds of wheat, the green Russian olive bush, and the beginnings of a hundred fruit trees from the seeds of those that had grown in their orchard in Tiegen. One of the boxes held the Kroeger clock whose pendulum would continue to tick away the hours of their future days in Manitoba. In another box was Aunt Lizzie's samovar that would never let them forget they had once lived in Russia. Grandfather Penner's encyclopedias were heavy. But Peter carried them as his special responsibility. Father's worn, black German Bible was in his jacket pocket. Before the day ended, he would open it and read a favourite passage.

Dusk came and a vast blue lake filled the landscape. "Lake Superior", a trainman called it.

By the next day the train was in the prairies.

"It's like the steppes of Russia!" Father was delighted.

Peter wondered if he would begin to sing on this speeding train with all the strange people sitting around them.

"I see a tumbleweed, Peter." Katya jumped from her seat as though to catch it in her arms.

Eventually the train slowed and stopped.

"We are in the city of Winnipeg," the Neufelds were told. They must board another Canadian Pacific train in the station and within thirty minutes would get off at the French-Canadian village of Giroux. "Your friends will meet you there," the trainman said in German. "It is the closest stop to Steinbach."

The Neufelds filled their arms with their possessions. Mother tied her black shawl securely about her head.

The second train was smaller and less crowded. Father and Peter piled all their baggage near the door. When the train stopped, they were the first passengers to step onto the station platform.

Father saw Cousin Cornelius at once. He was a tall, lean man with a thin rugged face, just like the photographs that had arrived over many years in letters from Canada. Aunt Esther, plump and smiling, stood beside him. Behind them appeared old friends and relatives from the Molotschna settlement. Some were in cars and others in sturdy farm wagons.

It's a dream again, Peter thought to himself. He recognized

150

Uncle Abraham and Aunt Helen Schmidt from the town of Morgenau along the Molotschnaya River. He and Father had almost stopped at their home once when they drove the buggy to Poltavaka many years ago to meet Otto at the railway station there. Now they were in Manitoba!

Katya began to wave at a tall man running towards them. It was Jacob Voth, the miller from Tiegen. His arms returned the wave, turning like the vanes from his old Dutch windmill.

Peter could almost imagine that Grandfather Penner was there, too, tapping his cane and shaking his wise old head with the billows of soft white hair.

The warm prairie wind roared around them and a giant tumbleweed bounced its zigzag way into Katya's arms.

"I've caught it!" she cried gleefully.

Then Cousin Cornelius approached Peter with a large white envelope that had his name printed across the front of it.

"It came by special delivery for you today, Peter, from your Uncle Jacob in Nebraska."

Father and Mother watched Peter open it.

Peter's eyes ran over the pages swiftly. At last the news was good. He wanted to shout and jump up and down. But he handed the letter to Father and asked him to read it aloud to everyone on the station platform. His full, deep voice could be heard even above the prairie wind.

Father read:

Dear Peter:
Now you can tell your parents about Otto. I know that Grandfather Penner asked you to keep the story a secret until your brother arrived safely in America.

Otto came yesterday to our home. He was thin and ragged and hungry, but he is well. He will write to you soon. The money from your Father's stove in Tiegen that you carried in your belt across the Russian border helped to buy his passage across the ocean. The good Dutch Mennonites put him on board a ship in Antwerp.

But he arrived in New York City with only 25 cents. He hitch-hiked across the United States and found our home.

It wasn't an easy job for a lad who knows no English. Soon you must visit us and we will visit you.

God bless you.

Uncle Jacob

Father placed his arm around Peter's shoulders.

"There will be time for questions when we get to the Dyck home. My heart is overflowing. Praise God that we are together and that so many of us are safe."

As the train sped away until it disappeared into the endless land, they walked arm in arm to the Dycks' farm wagon with the flared sides. It was just like the wagon that had carried them to the train in Lichtenau, South Russia, when the cherries were ripe in the orchards of Tiegen.

Notes

1. Father's statement on p. 83 ("If they come in spite of the rifles . . .") is taken from an article in the *Mennonite Brethren Herald,* p. 2, April 15, 1977. "Faith put to the Test" by David Dick.

2. The description of the wheat-and-dust meal on p. 103 comes from *Events and Experiences in my Life,* p. 34, by Agatha Wiens Nickel, Waterloo, Ontario.

3. Grandfather's answers on p. 120 derive from a conference of the Commission on Church Affairs at Alexanderwohl, Molotschna on Feb. 19, 1921 (60 villages represented) to chart a future course for Ukrainian Mennonites. *Lost Fatherland* by John B. Toews, Herald Press, 1967, p. 53.

4. The report about the teacher who said that the old God is dead (p. 122) is a direct quotation from Anna Dyck Martens, whose youth was spent in the Molotschna and who now lives in Winnipeg, Manitoba.

5. Father's letter on p. 122 was in fact written by a farmer to the *Canadian Mennonitische Rundschau,* 1925. Printed in *Lost Fatherland* by John B. Toews, p. 90.

Bibliography

Epp, Frank — *Mennonite Exodus*. Published for Canadian
   Mennonite Relief and Immigration Council by D.W. Friesen
   & Sons Ltd., Altona, Manitoba, 1976.

Hiebert, P.C. — *Feeding the Hungry* — Russian Famine
   1919-1925. Mennonite Central Committee, Scottdale, Pa.,
   1929.

Janzen, J. Henry — *"Greater Love Has No Man . . .Hamburg, S.
   Russia."* Published by the author in Kitchener, Ont.

Klassen, Aaron — *In the Fullness of Time*, English translation of
   German edition by Walter Quiring and Helen Bartel in
   Winnipeg, Manitoba. 1974 edition by Klassen in Kitchener,
   Ont.

Kornelsen, Mary — *A Few Excerpts from the Years 1914-1924*.
   Personal manuscript, Winnipeg, Manitoba, 1978.

Krahn, Cornelius, ed. — *From the Steppes to the Prairies*.
   Mennonite Publishing House, Newton, Kansas, 1949.

Lohrenz, Gerhard — *The Fateful Years 1913-1923*. The Christian
   Press, Winnipeg, Manitoba.

Lohrenz, Gerhard — *Storm Tossed,* a personal story of a Canadian
   Mennonite from Russia. The Christian Press, Ltd., Winnipeg,
   Manitoba, 1976.

Nickel, Agatha Wiens — *Events and Experiences in my Life*. Personal manuscript. Waterloo, Ont., 1976.

Reimer, Al., tr. — *Russian Dance of Death*. Herald Press, Scottdale, Pa., 1978.

Remple, Henry P. — *Passages Out of My Life,* Edwin Mellen Press, Toronto, Ont., 1977.

Rimland, Ingrid — *The Wanderers,* the saga of three women who survived. Concordia Publ. House, St. Louis, 1977.

Schroeter, Elizabeth A. — *From Here to the Pinnacles;* memories of Mennonite life in the Ukraine and in America. N.Y., Exposition Press, 1956.

Toews, John B. — *The Lost Fatherland* — The Story of the Mennonite Emigration from Soviet Russia 1921-1927. Herald Press, Scottdale, Pa., 1967.

Wiebe, Rudy — *Blue Mountains of China*. Wm. B. Eerdmans Publ. Co., Grand Rapids, Michigan, 1970.

Barbara Smucker, a Mennonite, lives and works as a librarian in Waterloo, Ontario. *Days of Terror* is the fruit of a vast amount of reading among actual accounts of the period. The author also interviewed many of the Mennonites who came to Canada and the United States in the 1920s.

Other titles by Barbara Smucker are *Henry's Red Sea, Cherokee Run, Wigwam in the City* (also published as *Susan*), and *Underground to Canada* (published in the United States as *Runaway to Freedom*).